The Black Swan

Black Swan

Christina Moore

Illustrations by Laura Boles Faw

Storm Petrel Publications

Citations

Surely, surely, slumber is more sweet than toil, the shore
Than labor in the deep mid-ocean, wind and wave and oar;
Oh rest ye, brother mariners, we will not wander more.

Alfred, Lord Tennyson, *Lotos Eater*, 1832

That faculty of beholding at a hint the face of his desire and the shape of his dream, without which the earth would know no lover and no adventurer.

Joseph Conrad, *Lord Jim*, 1900

"The Brandy Tree" (Otter's Song), Used with permission. Words & music by Gordon Bok, copyright 1967, courtesy of Timberhead Music, PO Box 840, Camden, Maine 04843. For additional information about the music of Gordon Bok please visit his website:

www.gordonbok.com

Library of Contress Control Number: 2006910948

ISBN 978-0-9791562-0-5

2 4 6 8 10 9 7 5 3

To Lir:

Who brings spirit to the sea.

To Sailors:

Who seek him at the gray horizon.

To Friends:

Here and beyond and those not yet met.

1: tunc *tempo: agitato*

I arrived with naught but lies.

Anticipation gone, rambling visions vanished while I confronted someone else's lost dream trapped in a floating hulk. I caught a hint of rot, sun-bleached mussels abandoned by the sea, baking on battered dock pilings. The ancient stain below a dumpster trapped light, still showing itself to be gooey and damp.

I felt a pungent flushing of embarrassment. I thought I had come east chasing my childhood. Wasn't I going to sea just as my father did, as my grandfather did, and as my great grandfather did? Yet, I wasn't stepping backwards in time; instead, I looked between dockside buildings at an anachronism.

The image of a ninety-foot sailing ship cradled next to a New England village was the same image they had seen: white lobster boats, dinghies, and mooring buoys. I breathed the same air they did. The odor of the place had not changed. I again breathed the air, scanning the barnacled granite riprap that fell away from the parking lot to the water's edge below.

My heart wanted to believe I was home. But no one greeted me. No one hugged me. No one asked me about my three days in the car.

No one probed gently about my husband. No one here remembered my mother, her sister, my father, or his father. I knew no one on this coast. Everyone I loved, I left behind.

I had not returned to the harbor and streams of my youth. Perhaps, I had confused my motives for coming here. At first, I admit, I came in pursuit of a lost youth. Standing there, I acknowledged a lost future.

I studied this schooner before me. Rust flowed down her bows like stains of old tears, undried, streaking down from her scuppers. My manifestations of hope collapsed, misshapen. They collided with the present.

This one hundred-year-old black schooner, dying quietly at anchorage, allowed me to savor the juxtaposition of reality and hope. Behind me, the village grew along the slope of a small hill. Defined by white church spires, stone piers, wooden docks, dinghies tied at the harbor's edge, the village rested in time yet had grown over three centuries. Nothing looked out of place, not even the rusting Toyota truck with a worn wooden bed. There were satellite antennas on roofs and people repairing ancient wooden lobster pots by hand. This was a place where people still rowed to get to their fishing boats, tapped the barometer each morning and evening, yet printed weather charts from the Internet. They took and kept what they wanted from each of the centuries.

Someone stepped up from behind me. "Are you the new cook?"

"Yes."

"She looks past her prime, doesn't she?"

"Yes."

"Do you have bags?" I turned to address this gentle-spoken man.

"My grandfather owns the Black Swan," he offered in explanation.

Neither of us moved. I returned my gaze to the harbor.

I saw movement on the deck; two men hammered the black metal. The sound was broken — not the sharp sound of a metal hammer on steel, but fuzzier and duller. They tapped and moved the hammer. Another puff of breeze carried a further reminder of all that surrounded me.

"How do I get out there?"

"You can get a hotel, you know."

"I could." I didn't move. "I won't."

"Okay." He echoed my resolve. "I'll help with your bags. Is this your Volvo?"

It was clearly from away: it had Illinois plates, the paint was shiny and clean, and the back was filled with luggage. Furthermore, I had parked it poorly.

"Yes."

He took the key that hung from my right hand to unlock the doors remotely. He returned the keys to the same hand. "At the risk of sounding foreboding, be careful out there. Be careful of that mate. I have never suffered a good thought about that man." He tossed my two sea bags onto the asphalt — "My name is Tad," — and closed the back of the car.

"Margaret." We shook.

Using a cane, Tad carried my two large bags to a boarding ramp, and I still hadn't moved my feet. I heard my own car horn toot twice. The men on the deck rose and saw me. They saw my bags. They saw Tad waving at them from my Volvo door.

A gray Avon inflatable motorboat wallowed its way toward us. It travelled the twenty yards across the harbor from the Black Swan's mooring. Tad slipped away when the two crewmembers approached, and I could hear them bickering.

"I told you she was the cook. I saw her first," the little one was saying to the taller one. "I saw her, and I knew that she was the cook. I told you that, remember." He had to yell over the outboard engine. They hit the floating dock. The dock jerked below me, and the inflatable dented in with such a force, it became clear how under-inflated she was. There were beer cans and stale water in the bottom of this boat. I gave a quick thought to my sea bags and their contents before the little guy tossed them into this swill.

I moved.

I walked down the ramp and toward this little craft. "Hey, are you the new cook?" He looked toward the taller man when he spoke.

"I am. Margaret Noonan." I offered my hand. Instead of accepting my hand, this kid elbowed his friend.

"Oh, hey, my name is David." David came to shake my hand, but I had already given up. "This is Joe. Joe, this is Margaret, the cook."

Joe mumbled something so softly I didn't hear him.

"No, I'll drive out," Joe again mumbled. I leaned in and watched his lips.

"You always drive." An argument started in front of me. I began to understand that there wasn't room for all of us. Back and forth these two went, until David took my bags out of the boat and got in. Then he pulled me in.

With me in the front of the Avon, she rode a little flatter across the harbor between the docks and the Black Swan. They drove around the far side and then slammed into the hull just below a boarding ladder. Both boys stood to help me up. I reached for the ladder with a firm grip and climbed away from them. The boat got unstable because I lifted my weight. David and the other one, Joe, stumbled backwards when the bow lifted, following my foot.

David started up after me. I turned to him and asked, "What about my bags?" I expected them both to go ashore and get them.

"They're fine. We'll show you around first."

A man met us at the side rail.

"Margaret, this is the mate. Sir, this is our new cook." I offered my hand again.

"Well, I like my breakfast hot: two eggs over medium, two pieces of bacon, soft. Coffee is always black and hot. I've had to do without toast. No one has ever gotten that stove to do anything right."

Now turning to David and Joe, he barked, "You two have stuff to do, don't ya? Still got that list?" They both looked at his legs, "Well do ya? What are you looking at? Do you have the list?" The mate dropped his right hand behind his back, elbow out. Both men reacted.

Joe spoke. "Yes, sir. I have it."

"Why didn't you say so? Learn to speak up. You mumble and babble like an idiot. Like those retards the state locks away." I saw the mate's right arm tense. His left shoulder rolled forward. The intensity of his focus narrowed to Joe's face. Joe didn't raise his arms in defense. He didn't flinch. He stood still, neither holding his ground nor running. Then his body relaxed slightly. He slumped instead of bracing for the blow I expected to see.

"Don't just stand there. There's only a couple of days to get this boat ready for sea, and you're both standing there like puppies waiting for a beating you deserve." The mate turned his back, walking aft.

I remained in place.

"Maggie." The mate gave a half-turn toward me. "You comin'?"

We descended the companionway into the galley, and the mate pointed out my bunk and the key points of the galley: stove, icebox, freshwater taps, seawater tap with foot pump on the sole—the grand tour of my new universe.

"After you get settled in and your stuff stowed, I'll show ya how to light that stove. It's a bit tricky."

I simply stared. The mate returned to the deck above.

This place was hell. The sole, or deck, was grimy. Dark, mildew-stained wood, food-encrusted dishes, and flatware littered every surface. A microwave sat on the counter with an extension cord heading toward the deck above, the nearest end wrapped in duct tape.

The odor mixed locker room, rot, soil, and every imaginable horrible smell.

I breathed slowly, letting my eyes adjust to the dim light. The more I saw, the more I wanted to run from the stained cupboards, rust, and filth, and I mean filth in the way my grandmother used the term: foul, putrid matter.

If I checked into a hotel, I really wondered if I'd be back. If I checked into a hotel, would the crew find me weak? Would they think I had run?

I breathed cautiously through my nose. The bilge smell was now appearing, an ancient and familiar smell. The bilge is the space at the very bottom of the boat. It becomes a harbor to dropped items, spilled items, seawater, leaking oils, and leaking fuel and has an odor that is normally overwhelming. It tempered the horror.

I toted everything portable to the deck. Everything from mattresses to pots went into a pile. From this pile, I pulled every bit of fabric. David and Joe hung from a board on the side of the schooner, beating the steel with a small hammer. Anger echoed with each hit.

I tossed the refuse into the bottom of the Avon. Anything cloth, anything trash, anything that had no value got tossed into the Avon.

I stacked all the other stuff together. I filled pots with water and flatware. I opened the microwave and rolled it on its back, exposing its mouth and throat to the afternoon sky. I gutted the galley and made two piles. Keepers went on deck to soak. Everything else went into that Avon.

Without a word, I started this little boat and headed to the dock. I filled my car's trunk with cushion covers, curtains from around my bunk, and dish towels. The rest went to the dumpster.

I placed my now-damp sea bags into the front seat of my car. They had remained on the dock all afternoon. Without explanation, I left. I left without another look and without a thought but disgust.

I returned the following day. The contents of the galley remained untouched during the night. The microwave was still gaping at the now-gray sky. Dew water pooled in the bottom.

I packed myself on board: four white five-gallon buckets, bottles of bleach, a case of sponges, a box of rags, a Costco-sized package of paper towels, metal wire brushes, bristle brushes, scrubbing pads of all sizes, and three boxes of three-mil trash bags.

The second day, I showed up with a high-gloss marine white paint, brushes, and blue gloves.

On the fourth day, I arrived with new cushions, mattresses, and freshly laundered everything. The crew had moved the Black Swan from her winter mooring to the dock.

I didn't make a noise when I found my sponges used around the boat. I bought more.

When I found one of my buckets had been used for thick, black oil, I bought another.

On that fourth day, I realized my personal funds were feeding an insatiable need of others. Like a dog in her neighborhood, I used a big, thick Sharpie marker to stake my territory: *GALLEY*; *DO NOT REMOVE FROM GALLEY*; *GALLEY*.

When I found a greasy hand print in my sink, I sought the crew out. They were near the bows, chipping rust with hammers. They'd chip, then paint, covering rust with sloppy, heavy coats of black paint.

"Don't touch my galley." These were my first words to them in days.

I walked away. I had spoken in anger. I wouldn't apologize.

On the fifth day, I brought my bags on board. Into clean drawers below my bunk, I stowed my clothing. Into the locker near the foot of my bunk, I hung my outside clothing: foul-weather gear, jackets, and heavy wool pants. I tucked a pair of sea boots away.

As I moved in, making further claims to my patch, regret started to creep into my heart. Wishing that I had been warmer and simply nicer to the crew, the words, "Don't touch my galley," replayed in my mind. A hazard of being alone in a small, confined world is that one's own words and actions echo and intensify with reflection.

Throughout my adult life, I have had little isolation. Long days at work included people talking to me, calling me, and e-mailing me. Evenings at home with my husband, Paul, consisted of television, meals, chores, and books. Music filled any silence during my waking hours. A surprise of my time alone was that I could experience, think, and evaluate processes simultaneously. I could judge myself from afar. Full sentences could form to discuss my activities, sentences never spoken, only heard.

The mate came down the companionway without a word. He stepped into the head.

I stopped working while I listened to him first pee, then moan and poop. I heard the toilet paper roll holder squeak. I heard the toilet pump squirt, filling, then emptying the bowl with seawater. When the mate finished manually pumping the toilet, I heard the D.C.-powered freshwater pumps kick on while he washed his hands.

He stepped back into my galley with a grin. "Looks good, Maggie." He gave a little step left and right, peeking around the area. "You ready for passengers tomorrow night?"

I didn't answer. I wasn't. I needed to buy food and think about cooking.

"Have you figured out that stove?"

No, I hadn't. I offered another blank stare.

"You got the state rooms cleaned up?"

Of course I hadn't. Didn't know I had to and wasn't about to admit that either. I flipped instantly from anger toward him to berating myself for allowing the mate to find any fault in my effort. How could I have known that the staterooms were for me to manage? Obviously, I'd have known by asking. I hadn't said a kind word to a soul since my arrival.

After the day closed, hours after the crew had retired to a bar, I marched on deck. I kicked the microwave over to drain water that had gathered in its throat. I hauled it to the side rail for a later trip to the dumpster.

I reviewed the afternoon's accomplishments: stateroom laundry dropped off, staterooms cleaned, menus planned. I thought about my clean galley. One more day to my maiden journey.

In cold water, I washed and brushed my teeth. I closed the curtain around my bunk for the first time. Then, with the small reading light on, I read the graffiti. It was carved into the wood and written on the wood that was the bottom of the empty bunk above me. The newer stuff, written in dark markers, was vile. The older material was fainter: dated and signed decades before.

Surely, surely, slumber is more sweet than toil, the shore
Than labor in the deep mid-ocean, wind and wave and oar;
Oh rest ye, brother mariners, we will not wander more.

As fickle as a woman to warm,
Yet rages as the devil's own bed.
She angers me so. Tepid coffee in a storm,
Then baking loaf after loaf of golden bread.
Roar on you iron witch
Heat me when I am hot,
Leave me to freeze when I am cold.
Aging shore-side, gone and old,
I will smile once, cursing you, bitch.

That faculty of beholding at a hint the face of his desire and the shape of his dream, without which the earth would know no lover and no adventurer.

I closed my eyes, lifting an old prayer into my heart, words that carried my mother's spirit into my mind. I held her hands. Her strength had failed with the years, although her voice commanded. Her turn of a phrase, her eyes, her hands remained as they were in my youth.

She understood work: intolerable, impossible work. She knew how to clean toilets and to cook. She understood the constraints the world placed on her. She didn't seek the education I did. She didn't have the opportunities. She warned me of the risks of working and living in the world of careers. She used a gentle tone and never discouraged my ambitions. She just tried to remind me of the risks I took.

"That's my fear. You do so well where you are. People leave you alone and the politics aren't too bad. If you move . . . "

"Mom, I am pretty good at it all. In fact, I like it."

"I know."

There was always a *but* lingering at the end of that statement, as if others were more skilled, better prepared, better trained, or simply had the family history in corporate business to advance. Actually, I have never understood her reluctance. I always attributed it to her own weakness for allowing others to dominate her. She would allow herself to get discouraged from exploring the world around her. She lived much of her life as if there were boundaries. She allowed herself to be constrained by the thoughts and actions of others.

I met the captain the following morning. He introduced himself to the passengers and thereby introduced himself to me. A slender man, dark beard, dark, tightly curled hair he kept groomed, he spoke quietly.

His small eyes moved through us. We each tied on a life vest. We each learned where the flares were located, the radio was located, and the names of the crew. Looking at me, he introduced me. I gave a little bow to the four passengers. I had a life vest on, well tied and done up right. Upon sitting, I hoped that the passengers mistook my efforts with the orange Mae West as a demonstration. I gracefully removed my vest when the others did, then gathered theirs from outstretched hands.

"Margaret, do you have anything to add?"

"No, sir, I don't." I offered a quick, professional answer to his unanticipated question.

"We'll get an early start tomorrow. There will be a hot breakfast in the galley at 7:30, and we'll pull away from the dock at 8:30. The evening meal is for you to enjoy here in town. Thank you." The captain walked away.

My first encounter with the captain came after six days and two nights on board. Never before had I seen him.

2. nunc *tempo: andante*

I look forward to the arrival of our passengers, ten folks for three days. During the first year, we'd leave port with two paying passengers, and then we'd ignore their interests. I didn't see it for a long, long time. My head was so stuck in that galley, the galley that I wore as carapace. If I heard "boo," I retreated like the ignoble turtle.

For this trip, like the last four, we have oversold each stateroom. Our brochure advertises accommodations for three in the staterooms. I will change that. The third soul typically sleeps in my galley. These are usually the youth, and for that I am grateful. I get bundles of bravado, hormones, and energy in my galley at night.

A family of three approaches the gangway.

"Hello, I am Margaret, your cook." The job expands well beyond the galley. I beam at these people coming aboard.

"Samuel, my wife, Linda, and our son, Calvin." Calvin is a geeky sixteen-year-old, pasty and flawed skin.

"Welcome, welcome." I shake the hands of each. I make the choice not to tell him that we'd had a Samuel on board once, a crewmember—a bit of historical editing. "Let me show you to your stateroom. You can stow your kit and familiarize yourself with the Black Swan."

From the galley companionway, we pass my bunk and the galley head and slip into the narrow corridor off of which the four staterooms are built. Samuel has to turn sideways in the corridor. Normal adult male shoulders will not fit in this space. The stateroom doors swing outboard into these tiny rooms. Most of these passengers own homes with walk-in closets that are larger than these staterooms. The rooms measure short of eight feet in length. The lower bunk folds up into the room with an extension board that allows it to approximate the size of a double bed. In its normal, narrow configuration, it is wide enough for a full-sized man to lie with his arms at his sides, snugly.

The lower bunk has a drop leaf much like a dining table. With the leaf down, it resembles a straight-backed sofa. Behind the cushions hide three clothing lockers. These cushions, like so much on a boat, pull double duty as back rests during the day and a mattress during the night. Below the lower bunk are four drawers. And the upper bunk is stepped back from the first. By following the curved flair of the hull, the upper bunk can provide the same comfort as the lower bunk, a bit more cave-like but comfortable. It does not have an extension leaf.

When a family of three packs into one of our staterooms, the parents sleep on the lower bunk and the child, on the upper bunk. When the child needed to go to the head, she would climb down onto the parental bunk. For this reason, children sleep in the galley, where there is loads of room and distance from parents.

Both bunks, upper and lower, have a lee cloth. During my orientation with Samuel, Linda, and Calvin, I hold up the mattress of the lower bunk. From under the mattress, I reveal a cloth that runs the length of the bunk. Samuel and Linda strain to look over. "A lee cloth is a clever, ancient device that will keep your body and your bunk together if the seas get fussy at us." I free the dingy canvas with blue trim from the plywood base of the bunk. "You take some small line such as this." I remove white, braided line from the drawer at my toe.

"Tie the line to these eyes here above. Climb into your bunk." I do this, not because these people are idiots, because it gets my body out of their way. "Then tie each of these four lines to these four grommets. Now, you may get kicked around, but you'll not land on the sole." I untie my demonstration, coil the line, and toss it casually into the drawer.

I fold the lee cloth back under the bottom bunk, and I explain, "Each bunk has a lee cloth. But if you choose to use the bunk extension leaf—and there is probably some fancy nautical term for all that, but I don't know it—then the lee cloth will be a barrier between the two folks."

Continuing, I add, "I am going to step out. Which means, I think, that we all have to step out." Linda turns aft, Samuel, forward. When Samuel sees that we have further trapped ourselves, he steps aft with his wife. Then they step into their room.

"When you're ready to call it a night, unclip the hatch." I point to a small hook-and-eye that holds the door fast against the partition in their room. "And close the door firmly. They don't really lock, but it is ugly and noisy when they swing and bang in the night."

I haven't figured out a way to address the form of the hatch itself. It is a standard door, hinges on one side and latch on the other. The bottom half has panels, but the top half is entirely louvered. It provides a visual privacy screen. The issue of sound-travel must cross the minds of couples thinking about a romantic time on the high seas, for sound certainly crosses the hatch.

Some couples clearly don't mind. I hear them. Some do mind, but their giggles and whispers conceal nothing. And then there are those quiet couples.

"Next stop on the tour is the head, a not very attractive name for a toilet onboard a ship." We step forward to the galley again. "At one point, people pooped with their fannies hanging over the bows of the ship, or the head of the ship." I figure anyone who has decided to take a vacation at sea has the fundamental bits of knowledge. Still, I try to fill in gaps.

"Now, there are a few steps in using this toilet. Failure to execute the steps properly will result in immediate turmoil." I pause. I never really want to get overly graphic on the consequences.

"First, add a little water to the bowl. Flip this lever and pump water in." Frankly, I don't do this all the time. "Not too much . . . about half full." Seawater foams when it moves about, an observation I made early on this job.

"Then do the business the gods sent you here for. Use as little paper as you can. I use it and fold it. If lucky, I fold it again and use it again. Of course, your hygiene is paramount to the process. I am only offering a few hints from someone who already knows the next steps. All of the organic matter and paper gets pumped by hand through small valves. Thirty or more pumps may be necessary. When done, flip the lever and pump dry. It is not a perfect system," I continue, "but flush and pump until the bowl is clean. When you are done, leave the bowl dry. Close the valve. The valve is closed when it is upright like this. Then pump until it is dry, like this."

I glance at my small audience. Many people know this drill. They have chartered in the Caribbean, own a boat, or cruised before. "Nothing but small amounts of T.P. and digested, southbound traffic. For northbound traffic, as it were, grab a bucket or a railing. No hygiene products and no trash. It will gum up the plumbing instantly." I look at the good folks for acknowledgement. "Yes?"

I get a "Yes" from Samuel when I look to him, a "Yes" from the kid, and one from Linda.

"Yeah, enough of that shit. The evening is yours. Explore the village, the Black Swan, and enjoy your night. Breakfast is casual but starts at 7:30."

While the parents walk away, I work to recollect the kid's name. "Calvin." He turns.

"Calvin, you are welcome to sleep in the galley. There is a bunk on the far side above the galley table. See it?" It really looks like a deep bookshelf to the uninitiated. "Teenagers and others come in here—a bit more communal but away from the parents. Behind the cushions, you'll find a locker similar to the one in your parent's room. Toss your kit in there."

"They're not my parents . . . well he is. She isn't." And he walks away.

I like their surliness. So many of our passengers are just so damned happy to be here that I can lose touch. A little angst is a good thing.

Ten passengers typically indicate that the galley will have another kid. I think a young boy or a teenage girl would be fun. Mix it up a bit. Bring Calvin out of his shell a bit. At this age, they change so quickly in a few days.

"My mother used to start all her meals that way."

Onions are sautéing in butter. There's garlic, chopped and staged for the heavy, large, cast-iron skillet.

"Can I help? What are you making?"

"Stew, beef stew." It did take me a while to accept the help of others. There isn't much space, and the work just isn't that difficult. "Come on over. Roll the beef chunks in that flour."

"What is that nutty odor?"

"Caraway." I toast caraway in the skillet with sesame oil. They pop and skitter all over the place.

"What's in the flour?"

"Salt and pepper, nothing very interesting, a little corn starch too. I have forgotten your name."

"Alicia."

We sauté the foundations, brown the meat. Then I open a screw top bottle that is marked *vinegar*. I take small swallow then pour about a half a cup in with the browned meat.

"Did you just drink vinegar?"

"No, of course not. A nice little Riesling. There are just too many rules. Can't cook without wines. So I tell myself, what's wine but a great vinegar? Our secret, eh?" It's a badly kept secret. The Coast Guard has these zero-tolerance laws regarding liquor on commercial boats, and real sailors and good cooks have ways around almost every one of those laws.

I dump the remaining flour and meat bits that I trimmed off into the slop bucket. "Let's do the carrots and potatoes. Just peel them directly into the bucket."

"Do you compost? My mother used to compost."

I hold any expression from my face. I had one passenger who asked me with her first steps in town what the elevation was. She was looking at the rolling green hills, clearly not cognizant of rock piers and tidal waters. I just said, "Well, ma'am, sea level, I guess." Saying such things during a nice slow exhale works better.

"No, composting is difficult. We feed the fish and seals."

"Sure, of course you would, huh? Tomatoes?"

"No, never. Two reasons, I guess. I don't like tomatoes in stew. That's number one. Second, I don't like serving food that has much acid. Some people at sea just don't need any more acid in the brew."

"I guess not. What's next?"

"That's it. Fresh bread from the afternoon is over there. We'll cover this with a little water and a lid. A couple of hours, and it'll be done."

"Want some help cleaning up?"

"Sure." It would have taken me as much time alone to wash as it took for two of us, but that isn't really the point. We don't have anywhere to go and nothing else really to do. I put a little water into a bowl, add about a teaspoon of bleach, and drop in a sponge. "Wash down the counters. I'll hit these dishes."

We can hear a few muted commands from the deck, then a flattening of the boat. The screech of the pulleys transmits through the boat.

"What's going on?" Alicia asks.

"We fell off."

"Fell off? Fell off what?" She doesn't look concerned or stupid. She does look like she's trying to make a joke of her lack of experience.

"Fell off the wind. We put the wind more directly behind us. We've eased the sheets, letting the sails out farther."

"Do you know where we are?"

"Probably. Winds out of the south, southeast. We're sailing pretty close to north. We are probably behind a couple of the islands, Ansebois or Ani-boy, as some say around here. Should we check? We're done here."

"Sure."

"Grab the slops, we'll dump those while we're on deck." One of the things I have grown to love on this job is that adults feel free to be children again, not just in their playfulness but also in their openness. They are willing to be led, to learn, to help. Forty-year-olds become eight-year-olds again and enjoy it.

Alicia has the slop bucket in her hands. She looks west, toward the coast of Maine. There sits the small cove named by the French hundreds of years ago, Ansebois, wood cove. She steps closer to the starboard rail, which is also the windward rail on this tack. I give a little verbal cue, kind of a *tsk* sound, then I give three more. She looks at me. I shake my head. I point toward the other rail with my thumb. She wrinkles her brow at me. I just nod again.

We approach the leeward rail at the same time. "Men learn this lesson early. Politely, we say, 'don't spit into the wind.' Men who don't learn the lesson, wet their own leg." She tosses the contents over the lee side, the side with the booms.

"The wind would have carried some of that back on deck or to the hull had you dumped on the other side."

"I see."

"If you ever have a question, spit. Or really, the cleaner way is to watch the wind. Typically, you'll dump on the lower side of the boat, the side with the booms. It becomes natural after a while." I take the bucket from her and walk away. I lay it at the galley companionway hatch on my way to the helm.

I smile at the captain, something I have become accustomed to doing.

"Hello, Captain."

"Hey, Cookie. Wha' cha doin'?"

"Burnin' gruel. Wha' chu doin'?"

"Laying a slalom course." The captain's wake, of course, is perfectly straight.

"Nice . . . hey, if I do this, I promise I won't hit any islands . . . "

"Sure."

This routine's as familiar to me as proofing yeast and lighting my stove. It feels a lot like flirting, and I don't think either of us minds. "Heading, sir?"

"Out there." He points over our bows, "That a way." The first time he said this to me, I wasn't sure I understood him exactly, but his smile gave it away.

I have learned that Kieran expects me to look at the binnacle and the wake, pick a good course, keep the sails full, and not hit anything. Our only formal destination is the dock from which we untied. We are not due there for days. Where we travel between departure and arrival is for us to decide.

I wink at Samuel and toss a smile to him playfully. "Where is your lovely wife?"

"I don't know." And it doesn't really matter. There isn't anywhere to go on a ninety-foot schooner.

"Is Calvin enjoying himself?"

"Seems to be. I think he is below the bowsprit now." This is a no-no but one that we enforce with discretion on this boat. The other young passenger is an eight-year-old girl, full of adventure and spunk. She has climbed everything and pulled on anything that was asked of her. Regrettably for Calvin, she isn't eight years older. She may have bowled over my shy, young, male teenager friend, but it would have been fun to watch.

"Are you enjoying yourself, Samuel?"

"Absolutely!" Samuel has tanned a bit. His eyes are a little clearer.

"Not bored?"

"Nope."

"Good."

Samuel scans the horizon. "Is she a new boat?"

Kieran and I look at each other. This comes to both of us as a compliment. In the past year, we have spent a great deal of time and some money on the Black Swan's luster. The paint is smooth and no longer looks like a job committed by a punished and resentful seaman. We've done a little sandblasting, scraping, fresh priming, and fresh painting. Items too rusted got cut out and new bits welded back in. I look to Kieran, wondering who should answer the question. We both know to what conclusion this conversation will come.

"No, no she's not." Kieran lilts a bit more as he often does when he starts to tell a story. If he smoked a pipe, this is where he would pull the pipe from his vest and tamp it.

"How old is she?"

"Turn of the last century."

"Really." The surprise is genuine, as it normally is. "What was she built for? Doesn't really appear to be a fishing vessel . . . "

"You're right about that. She wasn't a fishing vessel, far from it. In polite society today, we'd refer to her occupation as import/export and wink as we said it."

"Oh . . ." He ponders a moment. " . . . smuggling."

"Yes. In her day, she was fast. Faster than most, and she knew these waters. It's a short run to Canada. It is relatively easy run to Saint Pierre and Miquelon, which are still territories of France. There's no telling the cargoes she ran. We know that liquor was a staple for years. With remnants of the Spanish-American War, then First World War, then Prohibition, there was ample need for goods that could be brought in discreetly and quickly. Was then, still is." Kieran nods to me and gives a half-wink.

"We have been collecting stories of this lady ducking in and out of these islands, well before radar or loran, using their wooded coasts as cover while she played hide-and-seek with revenuers and Coasties.

"There are stories of this lady dumping her cargo over the side in wooden crates, crates weighted down with solid salt, big boulders of salts sewn loosely into sacks of canvas. She'd get skittish when she saw a revenue boat on her horizon. She'd dump and run. Twenty-four hours later, she'd return to find the cargo happily bobbing on the surface just waiting to be hoisted on board. The salt dissolved, the weight gone, the crates with cork and wood carried their cargo of sealed bottles to the surface."

I, too, can imagine the excitement of a chase, a chase made by two sailboats. Both would be masters and victims to the wind, the tides, the currents, the shadows, and swirls left by the trees on land. Success would go to the faster boat, the more knowledgeable skipper, the more adept crew, and a little bit of luck. With the introduction of engine-powered boats, the advantage of speed would give way to reliability, range, skill, and intrigue. I think that radar and aircraft were probably the first great blows suffered by the Black Swan. World War II and fashion were the next insults. Everything modern was cherished, the old ways tossed aside. Today's fashions still play against her to some extent; she is a steel schooner, plying the wind jamming trade, a trade dominated by vessels of wood. The wood brings greater romance, greater mystique, and stronger ties to history.

"What's burnin' down there?"

"Nothing. We're having beef stew."

"Again?" Kieran is a poor whiner. Even when he tries, he can't. There isn't a lot of variety in my food. I just don't have the resources at sea. I don't have refrigeration nor fancy cooking techniques. I have fresh bread every day, hot meals three times per day, homemade soups, salads—at least for the first days of a cruise—wonderful cuts of meat, homemade pastas, seafood dishes. I stir it up a bit. You'll not find nouvelle cuisine in my galley or on my plates. Instead, you'll find *cuisine ordinaire*, normal, old-fashioned, home-cooked food.

"Cookie, should we pull behind Rodel Point?"

"It's as good a place as any to drop the hook." I don't tell the old stories to the new passengers. Rodel Point is a location well known to this old girl.

Without television, life takes on an older rhythm. This is a cruise ship without a climbing wall, nor a fleet of noisy, mosquito-like jet skis, nor nine ballrooms of entertainment and buffets. *Hanging from the hook,* a term we use to describe being at anchor, becomes quiet. People will sit on the deck near the wheel. Couples will cuddle, finding warmth. Memories of old vacations to a mountain cabin are recalled and retold. Stories of parents reading aloud to pre-teen children are remembered.

During the day, people will tell jokes at the wheel. In the evenings, during what I call story hour, the pace slows a bit. Jokes are rarely told. I have, unsuccessfully, tried to introduce singing to this little ritual. I thought, what a fine time to pull out the old songs! I had been wrong. It doesn't work. Conversation flows like evening breezes: gently, in swirls, small starts, and periods of quiet.

"Linda," I speak quietly. "I have been seeing you write."

"Scribbling more like, I guess. I find it easy here."

I let the silence return, but she picks up her own thread. "I found myself writing a little poetry again."

"Oh, that's wonderful."

Samuel, her husband looks at her, surprised. He holds her in tighter, using their cuddle to give a warm and encouraging hug.

"Is it anything you'd want to share, have a few people listen to?"

"I don't know, hadn't thought about it." I am fascinated by the lessons and impulse people take on the Black Swan; sea, free time, no cell phones, and decent rest are all ingredients that nourish the mind, allowing people to revitalize ancient promises.

Linda slips from Samuel's embrace. Returning from the stateroom, she carries a yellow piece of paper and a flashlight. She hands the light to Samuel.

She begins: "I am calling it 'Spectrums.'" After an awkward, timid clearing of her throat, she reads:

"Red to violet
Infrared to ultraviolet
Courage to fear
Action, inaction
Love, and fear
Passion, contentment

"Nothing stands alone. No thought exists without context
No context without contrast.

"To address love, define courage.
As for loneliness, who can know what rests far on that spectrum?
To define courage, think about a single step.
What shall that step span?
What span left unstepped, shall never again be
And yet, the horizon rests, uncaring beyond our reach

"To explore fear, address love
Oh to say with word without fear. The very word a lament:
what is it to feel love without regret?
who can know love without shame?
Introduce yourself to love; thereby find mortality;
Death, loss, violence, abandonment, even growth,
the gentlest caresses of love, changes love.

"Why must we bear each morning with a memory of yesterday?
Dawn has no history. Yesterday's clouds don't exist.
Yesterday's sun is a different sun. Today's storm will come.
An ocean can't remember a wave, nor the sky a bird.

But who would want that emptiness, a soulless existence?

"Give me one memory of a touch and I shall cry with an everlasting sorrow."

Tad meets us all at the dock again.

Some of the debarking passengers hug me. I work at avoiding the clichéd comments of pilots and flight attendants, but sometimes, I just can't. Twice a week, we stand at the dock, giving passengers a fair-thee-well. I accept their thanks with a trained politeness while offering kind words of company and appreciation for their enjoyment of my galley. Phrases such as "b-bye now," "bye-bye," and "see ya," escape my lips during the solemn occasion. With little variability, my mind focuses on the next trip, the next group, and the next series of meals.

Tad gets a wave from my hip. The black lab at his side is pulling on the leash, eager to run up the gangway.

"Raven!" The dog runs straight for me. I bend down to greet her. "You're such a good girl." I let her tackle me, and then I roll her over. She runs a full lap on the deck.

I offer Tad my left hand while he makes his last step, transitioning from the gangway to the deck. "Any progress?"

"A little."

"Good."

He lets go of my hand to walk aft.

Tad calls down the aft companionway, "Captain?"

3. tunc *tempo: agitato*

Anticipating a clear night with nearly full moon on my birthday, the afternoon's freshness corrupted. Green clouds turned the gray sea near black. Seeking shelter from developing winds that came from the south, we hid on the north side of Grimsay Island. With darkness attacking, the wind backed until it came off the ocean from the east, exposing us. We lay revealed when protection was required.

The chaos of movement disturbed everything: my stomach rebelled; the galley clanged; the Black Swan fought her anchor. Like an angry, punished child, she fought her tethers, fought to respond naturally to the abounding furor.

Never having known sickness at sea, I ignored symptoms and tried to relax in my bunk. When I understood that I was to vomit, I had just the time required to direct it to the sole. Retching again, I soiled the sneakers below me.

With a quick effort to dress, I scampered into boots, slicker, and sou'wester.

I faced forward, directly into the teeth of the rain. Out of my bunk, on my feet, the nausea subsided. But my throat burned, and my ego was damaged. Rain poured from the cuffs of my jacket, flowing down my fingers in a stream. *Landsman. Landlubber.*

Sick.

I stepped to the transom. The black water was glass in the lee of the wind.

Elsewhere, the wind decapitated waves. Waves curled, rising, creating instantaneous valleys of calm before the wind carried crests into the air. Wind created upward driving rain. In this flurry flew a small bird, nearly dark with a bit of white on its rump. It found ways of landing on the fleeting leesides of waves. To depart, it would crest a wave, spread wings, and launch into the wind, but in a blink, it would turn, flying with the wind. I wanted to believe it did an aerial flip, but I don't think the facts will support me. I was watching a black bird in a black night playing in the foam and spray of the worst violence I'd seen at sea.

With bladder full, stomach knotted, and throat burning, I held everything in. When the pain crescendoed, I could not return below. I held. And I held. Water poured from my leggings as it did from my sleeves. Wet in, wet out, I sat on the cuddy top. The warmth of my urine soothed when it flowed down my long underwear and into my boot. There, it mixed with cold rainwater. There it sat.

We were at sea with but two passengers, a load so light I could not understand how the costs of the trip were covered. There the passengers were, with me, whipped by rain and tumult. They suffered greater misery and greater pain than I.

Too afraid of my own stomach, I remained on deck well past any sense of misery, chilled feet shriveled in wet boots, hands numb to ribbons of water cascading down from my shoulders.

During the night, the wind continued to back, continued to build. Come morning, wind howled from the north, pushing us toward a rocky beach.

A day later, we were anchoring off Rodel Point. As seemed to be part of the routine, we dropped the hook about an hour before sundown. A faint lilac fragrance carried in the breeze. The breeze was a mixture of warmth and coolness, like the brown and white swirls of a parfait, an incomplete blending of land and shore. I turned west-southwest to find the fading heat of the sun and felt a shiver run down my spine. A seal barked, and a dog gave a lazy half-howl. I walked around the galley hatch, inventorying the world. An orange buoy seemed out of place. Joe was on the bowsprit with a passenger, furling the headsails. David was securing the main's boom in its crutch, the captain, out of sight, as usual.

Without the mate on deck, I felt comfortable to sit on the hatch next to the mast. I remembered a story from a Swedish friend in college. On sunny days, warm enough not to chill the skin, teenagers would quickly strip to their underclothing and perch themselves, facing the sun. I always pictured it as speed tanning. With these images in mind, I undid several buttons on my flannel shirt, closed my eyes, and relaxed.

I felt little stabs of anxiety with every movement on deck, a sense of being vulnerable and exposed. I fought to keep my eyes closed while people moved past me. I worked to identify individuals by their step, their actions, the sounds they made. Much of being on a schooner was still unfamiliar to me.

The basic operations of sailing had become routine: anchoring, tacking, sails up, sails down, the starting of the engine, the silence of the engine being shut off. I paired ancient nautical terms with specific noises and activities. Since I rarely had the perspective of the deck, I used imagination to see this boat sail. I had seen and participated in every evolution and knew the meanings of "stand by to come about," "helm's alee," "loose and haul away," "lively now," "horse it in," "'attle do," "make it fast." I smiled, thinking of how *lively* meant *fast* and *fast* meant *tied* or *fixed.*

Quick's first definition is *not dead, alive.* To do something quickly is to do it with life, lively. *Fast* seems rather the opposite in this little steel island called the Black Swan. "She's holding fast," simply means the anchor has a firm grip on the bottom. In this drowsy state, I wondered what the phrase, *she is fast*, would mean: moving or not moving? Like the word *cleave*, which has two opposite meanings simultaneously: to cut apart and to join together. My musings entertained me in my drowsy state.

I heard the aft companionway open and stiffened, but I told myself to remain still, to keep my eyes closed. Silently, I said, *I am safe and entitled to this spot of sunshine, and I am near to my galley. I am not a dog to be chased to her own yard when another dog appears.*

"David," I heard the mate in a hushed tone. "Get a hook on that buoy. Make it fast." I chuckled. His tone was almost gentle, and that he spoke to my thoughts brought me some comfort. Maybe I was wrong about him.

I sat up. I sleepily opened my eyes to watch Joe and David hook and haul the buoy on deck. They tied a line to it, then dropped the orange ball over the side again. Eventually, they tied it all off forward near the anchor. I looked around for a passenger to talk to and entertain myself with. I still had twenty minutes before I needed to address the next phase of dinner.

Standing, I spied yet another of my kitchen sponges in a dirty bucket.

I hadn't yet completed a month. Nothing in my corporate life had prepared me for this environment. Even the stories my father told me about the cruel sea and the men that sail her didn't reconcile with what I was seeing here every day. I had heard stories of horrible captains and brutal sailors, but in a town like this, people are neighbors. In the modern age, there is a functioning police force. There are labor laws. There are state boards, committees, the Coast Guard, and none of this explained the behavior of this crew and this mistreated vessel.

Going back to Illinois was an option but not one I was willing to accept, not yet. Too much had happened. I hadn't left well. And returning would be accepting a defeat I was not ready to accept. I could not. I'd lost everything: first my mother, then the job, then Paul. I became the object of pity. Paul would meet me at the door to our house. "Oh sweetie, I am glad you had an adventure." I hadn't had any previous setbacks in my career. I could go back, but that would be it. I'd attained my highest mark. I'd shown my weakness and fumbled. I'd run away and limped back. Pity pisses me off.

My grandfather sailed these shores his entire life. My father died at sea, fishing off this coast. I was born of this stock; I belonged here, probably better than I belonged anywhere else. At least, the forces I dealt with were real.

The sea is real. The wind is real. These paying passengers are real. This crew couldn't get in the front door of any corporation: they expose every thought, every bit of violence, every intention, for all to see. There is no hypocrisy here.

I had seen my share of white-collar foolishness. Although I'd never participated, I understood and saw the crimes that erode trust, tumble trading markets, and eviscerate pensions. We'd all discussed the hubris of the people committing these crimes. We all knew. Some bragged on the chutzpah of these executives while the dirty crimes involving drugs, battery, and theft existed in a different universe. Those were the real bad guys.

From the galley, I heard David and Joe untie us from the orange mooring buoy. Within moments, we were under power, steaming out of the small harbor. I heard the passengers' feet moving to assist the boys in hoisting the sails.

During one of our many shore days, I decided to try my hand at baking bread. Why shouldn't passengers on a New England schooner expect fresh-baked bread? It is what I would want. The options at the grocery store were vast, but packaged foods are fragile. Breads got stale, or wet, or absorbed odor. I reviewed the *Joy of Cooking* to identify the needs: flour, yeast, salt, eggs, and oil. I decided to substitute canola oil for melted lard. I fired up the stove with a few small wads of newspaper and a bit better understanding of how to handle the beast.

Upon my return from the store, I prepared myself for a massive production. The stove was up to temperature. I laid out the ingredients on the bleachy-washed surfaces. Then I started: *Scald one cup milk.* With the precision of a chemist, I followed the instructions. I got the temperatures to eighty-five degrees when called. At first, the dough resembled a pot of paste. It all just stuck. Long tendrils of dough adhered to the bowl's edge and my wooden spoon. My spoon lost its shape. Flour and dough caked to it. It grew larger and larger, becoming something like a paddle. Diligently, I kept adding flour until the dough transformed into a springy mass, a form. It stuck to itself and started releasing from the bowl edge. I tossed the spoon into the sink before I mixed by hand.

Following the directions, I covered the bread for fifteen minutes. Then I folded, kneaded, and folded the dough. With a moist dishcloth, I covered the bowl for a two-hour rise. The mess I made took some thirty minutes to clean, but I could see then that a lot of that mess was the result of my inexperience. I was already envisioning short cuts and steps to eliminate, such as sifting the flour in great piles on the counter. A quick tack or a sudden wave would strew flours to the dark corners of this galley and coat the galley sole.

I cleaned my mess. I read my book and watched the magic of bread rising. It was as if the bowl itself got pregnant. I imprinted my fingers repeatedly, finding that it was only seventy-five minutes of rising—not the full two hours *Joy* called for. The imprints of my fingers lasted. When I punched the dough down, it deflated. It hissed; it encased my hand while it fell. I folded, punched, and gave a quick kneading in the bowl. I made no mess with this kneading process. I gave it a second rising and prepared the loaf pans I'd bought with a little oil.

I was regretting not having adventured further to explore heavier, heartier breads with whole wheat flour and a few seeds. The decision I made when reviewing the recipes was to start with the fundamentals.

Having seen these steps, I felt ready to leap forward into the darker, richer flavors.

I baked the loaves until they were the flaxen blond of an August wheat field. I cut one loaf immediately, and covered a piece in butter. I ate one piece while I eagerly cut the next. Pools of hot butter formed on the pieces while I held them. Butter dripped into the sink while I stood eating one piece after the next.

Paul would enjoy this bread and enjoy seeing me have this fun. I am not sure that bringing homemade bread into the office would do anything but cause some confusion. I was no iron maiden, no dragon-lady boss, just a basic VP-boss. I got better funding than most. I tended to grab interesting projects. Funding and opportunity brought loyalty from employees.

Here? This was a different world. I decided then to find some of the best bread books and bake bread at sea—breads that would be a hot meal in the hand, breads that would nourish, sate, and bring out relationships and companionship.

4. nunc

tempo: adagio

I awake in stillness and solitude.

I don't look at my watch. It is between four forty-five and five A.M. — a routine since my first nights aboard. For years, I required an alarm clock to get me up at six, a noisy reminder to rise and hit the gym, the shower, and the office.

In the dark of my mornings on Black Swan, I discover a quiet, the silence of a mind at work in a world at peace. Movements manifest sound, each action illuminating an imaginary landscape: water on a steel hull; breezes in the rigging; creaks and groans from an old ship; the patter of small feet, most not human; birds meeting the dawn; seals vocalizing; the odd whale. In this concert, I can hear weather. With fog, sounds are deeper. Shrills and high pitches are truncated. Distant sounds travel farther. Near sounds are muted. With clear air, the morning sounds brighter, crisper. Wind transmits through the hull. Rain dances on the decks. Waves roll me. This is an ancient quiet.

The Black Swan rolls, stirring the galley.

These hours are mine. No matter who may have slept in my galley, a teenage passenger, a stray from a bar one of the crew allowed on board, an apprentice cook, or a black dog, they remain silent during my morning mass.

Awake.

Awake in bed. Not wanting to return to sleep, not yawning, not rushing forward to meet a day that hides an hour from the east's horizon. I inventory my blessings. I pray. I remember people who have blessed my life. I plan my meals. The tempo of my day finds cadence with my breathing, rhythm of my heart. Each beat is strong, distinct yet flowing, one to the next, bound by frail tension. Counting these beats—one from the ribs, one from the diaphragm—my breath eases further. My legs stretch into the cold reaches of my bunk, and my body uncurls. My arms find their places by my sides, then cross my chest. My chin comes free from the blankets.

I breathe deep, not counting, not inventorying in the traditional manner, but assessing how I will approach the day. Each breath, each beat is a reminder to cherish.

Life is not found in the presentation of the food I put on the table or the glamour of my galley but in the grace I discover within the galley. I lift my heart with my own words:

May I discover the grace in each movement.
May I reveal that of grace within.
May I recognize the grace of others.
Shall peace find those I meet.

I restore dreams to my imagination. I cherish the lulling caress of the boat.

I move.

No matter how cold, I hold back the first gasps. One layer, two: socks, sneakers. I turn to pull the toilet kit from the little bookshelf on the far side of my bunk. I don't wash early in the morning. I pee, brush my teeth, and take a drink of cold, fresh water. Washing comes later. It comes with the warm water, heated by the stove.

I bestow the morning with ritual. There's nothing more ritualistic than lighting the stove.

Lighting the stove joins me with my mother's mother and her foremothers. I can never think about the difficulties of lighting my stove without homage to people who lit a stove without a match, without a shred of paper. What must it have been to warm a house, make meals, and bake bread from an ember carefully buried under ashes?

I don't have to bank embers. I don't have to cut kindling. I do have to contend with water in the fuel, crud in the fuel line, kludged technology, and a stove so massive that only after hours of steady attention does it become capable of cooking.

"Good morning." The stovetop is both cool and dry.

Whether for scientific, spiritual, or practical reasons, I touch the stove when I greet her. Cast-iron, dropped into place during the construction of this ship, the stove, over a century old, weighs hundreds and hundreds of pounds. Once it burned coal, wood, kerosene, and probably gasoline. It burns any fuel source. At present, it burns mineral spirits. Given fuel, heat, and adequate oxygen, it will warm. A wet stove won't light well. A wet oven foretells trouble.

The primary fuel valve rests on the far left near the mast. The fuel line is constructed from standard, copper, water-plumbing parts. There is a valve like the one found in most basements. This fuel line is a length of crooked, poorly supported copper piping. I open the valve, which allows the fuel to flow from the barrel located on the deck down the pipe. This valve I turn three full revolutions: one, two, three.

I bend and open the secondary fuel valve. This valve opens the path to the plastic float-valve carburetor. Clearly not designed for being at sea, this carburetor must have been a part of a home heating system, maybe for domestic fuel oil. The fuel from the deck fills the carburetor's belly, then trickles into the bottom of the firebox. Here, a brick has been cut with a molded circular pool. This hole becomes a small fuel reservoir. The brick first dampens, then floods. With the lid off the firebox, I watch.

I decide there is enough fuel. Too much and the fire will drown. Too little, it won't light. Sated, I tear a complete towel from the roll of paper towels. This, I twist into a loose rope. Too tightly, it won't burn completely. Too loose, and it burns too quickly. I light the towel.

It burns. It warms the fuel. The fuel starts to evaporate. This gentle gas burns coolly, warming the air in the firebox, evaporating more fuel. Although flammable, mineral spirits is a fuel capable of extinguishing a lit match and not igniting. It is a fickle fuel.

After minutes, I turn on the blower and feed the tender fire oxygen.

Behind the stove rests a neatly coiled set of copper pipes and a cistern. In two hours, hot water will flow into my galley without the aid of pumps. Cold water flows from a blue plastic barrel on deck into this cistern, warmed by the stove. From there, it flows to my sink.

During the moments that the sky fades from black to deep blue, my galley stove roars. The galley warms, and a horizon appears on the deck.

On to bread: water warms in a cast-iron Dutch oven; yeast, I cut three packets with a pair of scissors; sugar; three eggs I beat in a bowl; butter melts in a warming cast-iron skillet. Both the skillet and Dutch oven rest directly over the fire. The rest of the stove is cold to the touch. A brown foam starts in the Dutch oven.

I pull big plastic tubs from under benches at the galley table. These are the largest Tupperware-like stuff I could find, must be seven gallons each—one for white flour, one for whole wheat. I drag the bins to the galley. Stirring the proofing yeast with my fingers, I wait.

Then I add the eggs and the proofed yeast to a large stainless bowl. I add flour by the cup. I don't count—just add. Then I stir. If it is too sticky, I add flour. And I stir. I stir until I can't stir, and then I use my hands. Mixing, stirring, kneading, I make a large ball of light brown dough. I pull the ball from the bowl and work it further. If it gets sticky, I dust with flour. A practiced hand and an experienced eye guide me. The nibbles I take discover the balance of salt to sugar, sweetness to richness. Gone are the milk, the piles of flour, and the books. Gone is the hesitancy.

I then wash my bowl. I coat the inside lightly with grapeseed oil. Into this bowl, I toss the firm ball of dough. I wet a tea towel and wring it with a few strong twists. I find the corners, then shake it like a blanket. A little snap echoes in the galley; a small spray hisses on the stove. I cover the dough, retiring it now for the first rising. The bowl rests near the middle of the cool stove. With the firebox on the extreme left side, the stove warms from left to right. In an hour, I will still be able to touch the iron below the bowl without burning my hand. In two hours, the entire top will be very hot.

Stove lit, bread started, I head to the deck. I love to watch the sun rise. There's nothing to do in the galley—no one to feed, not yet.

After sunrise, I think about people. I don't explore the sadness of my early years. No, I think about the people I will meet. I think about the next time I will lie next to a fireplace, cognac, somber colors, and a warm library in the winter. I don't think about sex directly, but the afterglow, the anticipation, the companionship. All the benefits, all the love, I look forward to that moment. The contrast to the chills I feel when I stir invigorate me. *To taste cognac from lips of another, humm . . .* There's no violence here, no. This thought carries me to chocolate, rich, dark chocolate with a hint of cinnamon and spice, chocolate served to me from warm fingers.

I lie back to catch the last of the stars on in the western sky. Mars is passing Orion's belt; Venus is low; one horn of Taurus is missing in the fading darkness. I see the delicate peak of a rising crescent moon.

This is the last morning of this cruise. We will haul anchor and sail back to the harbor after folks stir.

After I serve breakfast and folks head to the deck for their last day of sailing, I continue my routine. I know the run is about three hours. We will do it in six. Folks return to town after a day of sailing. They will be driving back to Boston or wherever they came from. If people have long drives, we allow them to stay the night on board.

Last Day, as I call it, has its own character. I don't make dinner. Lunch is a selection of everything that is left: pork sandwiches, prime rib sandwiches, pea soup, and onion soup, dibs and dabs of what I find in the icebox. Passengers get to return to their favorite meal. Of course, hot, fresh bread awaits the noon meal.

The time I would normally use for preparing for dinner, I use for cleaning. I pitch anything that is open from the icebox; Seal Food, I call it. I wash the icebox with bleachy water. I sort and clean the food lockers.

"Stand by to come about."

The boat is listing about ten degrees to starboard, tilting everything toward the hull, my right. I turn and spread my arms in front of the rows of spices with freshly washed tops.

"Helm's alee."

The schooner turns under my feet and flattens. People run, sails flap. She comes through the wind. As she builds speed, she heels down to port. Spices lie against my arms. I ease everything to the edge of the counter. Unlike the counters in homes, this counter has a two-inch board running around it. It stands above the counter with oblong holes that allow liquid spills to flow to the sole, then to the bilge. This fence acts to hold small items or heavy items on the counter. Regrettably, it can also act as a trip, launching articles such as spice containers and milk jugs from the counter with an overhead rotary motion.

With the Black Swan once again stable, I relax. The spices are at rest again. I lay them up, one at a time, back behind the elasticized netting that makes up the front of my cupboards.

I make small notes in my journal. This black and white composition book is my shopping list, recipe book, guide, and memory. Simply called, *the cook's log*, I can easily go back through it and read about the last three years. There are few editorials in my notes. Yet, I've recorded the impact of each experience.

"Stand by to rig preventers."

This command tells me that we are going to pull off the wind. The massive booms will get secured when we sail with the wind near our back. Kieran has decided to take a circle tour of Carinish. One simple command, and I can know his thoughts. One movement, and I know our path. This is not the boat and the crew I first came to sea with.

6010861

5. tunc *tempo: allegro*

"No, Paul, it wasn't that bad. We were in a little cove. There wasn't anything to worry about. It was just a storm. "

"Got wet. Got tossed around a bit. Lost a night of sleep. Maybe, in hindsight, it'll be fun. I don't know."

"No, I'm going to stick it out."

"Of course I don't have any regrets. It is a little lonely without friends to talk to, but I think I need the quiet time. It's good for me, don't you think?"

When I returned the cell phone to the glove box in the Volvo, I thought about taking a drive. The idea waned. *These roads are not good for a fast drive anyway; some slow pickup truck or RV just in the wrong place or a village appears around a corner.* I was surprisingly eager to get off the phone with my husband.

During the last year at work in Illinois, our department started with some new sayings. Sayings take on a life in a corporation. They become slogans, and people come to accept some complexity or change or risk. Our recent saying was: "Hope is not a strategy."

There I sat in the passenger seat of my Volvo, seeing some of the lies I'd told myself. The success of my summer and my sabbatical relied on hope: hope for change, hope for friends, hope for better weather, and hope for a decent crew.

There it was: the hope factor.

June had started. My forty-fourth year had started, started in fact as my life started, I guess: naked, cold, wet, and covered in my own excretions.

June had started, and I didn't know my bosses' names.

June had started, and I didn't know the captain's voice.

June had started, and I didn't have a clue what kept this rusted schooner sailing day after day.

June had started, and I wasn't ready to see myself dressed in a suit again, not yet.

For weeks, I had stood in conversation, waiting for someone to use the mate's name. I waited for the moment when he'd introduce himself. I waited. I never asked. I rested on hope.

Thus, I became charged with a mission, several in fact, for I didn't know the captain's name either. I hadn't seen the fo'c'sle. I had never been to the aft quarters where the mate and captain each had staterooms and a shared head. For that matter, I had never seen the engine. It was time to put names on the people and places in my world, to see them, to learn them, and to understand them.

I had to get the mate's name. I needed his name but would not give him the satisfaction of being the ass if I asked him directly. He'd lord over me. He'd have something I'd want.

No, the trick was to find his name, then use it. I'd own his name with that. Knock him down just that one notch. *Where does one find a name? How do I do this without him knowing of my efforts?*

The mate's truck with Maine plates was within sight. It was in the same parking lot where I sat in my Volvo. I wrote down the plate number and walked to the library.

A few minutes on Google, a toll free call, and a quick, forty-dollar charge on my credit card, and I had his name, Samuel Selby—Selby, a plain English name.

Little Sammy. Sammy the shit. Sammy, the little tyrant.

I walked into the town hall to pursue the captain's name. Little signs extended into the hallway, a décor that reminded me of the 1930s, although all looked clean and new. The granite was in great shape. There was no musty odor, and the lighting was great. Signs read: *Town Clerk*, *Selectmen*, *Water Board*, *Vital Records*, and *Police*.

The police sign was at the far right end of the building. It was to their door that I walked.

"What is the name of the captain of the Black Swan?"

"Don't know, really." The officer turned to the interior of the office, "Anyone know the name of the captain of the Black Swan?"

"Who's askin'?"

"Don't know." He shrugged toward me.

A youngish man approached the countertop. "Do you know him?"

"I guess so," I answered. "I work with him."

"You're off the Black Swan?"

"Yeup."

"What do you do?"

I answered him. I didn't really care, but it appeared to me I was about to admit that I didn't know my boss's name. "I am the new cook . . . . " I waited a few beats. "It's a bit embarrassing. No one has ever used his name, and he has never used it. And I'm getting curious. I just want to know his name."

"How long have you been on board?"

"A few weeks." I designed my answer to protect my ego and shortened my time down a bit from two months. He studied me, exposing his curiosity and wondering about his next move.

"Who are you?"

"Margaret Noonan. I'm from away, but I was born here. My family was from near Bath before they moved to Illinois."

He studied my face, watched my eyes. "Would you put your hands up here on the counter for me?" I clenched my fists at my sides.

He waited.

Still clenched, I waited. *He has want I want. And I haven't a clue where his thoughts are taking him.* I yielded, placing two hands with fingers spread on the counter between us.

"Can you roll up your sleeves?" he asked while he examined one hand, the back and the space between my fingers. Then he smelled my fingers. His nose poked at my hands like hen on corn: sniff, sniff, sniff.

"You are a curious fellow," I offered.

"Cautious, I'd like to think."

"I haven't been sniffed in public in a while. Well ever, I think, 'least not by a human. A few dogs have approached, but . . . . " Neither of us acknowledged my failed attempt at humor.

With that, he carefully plucked two of my hairs from the wool of the men's overshirt I wore. These he put into an envelope. His odd nature and his nonthreatening attitude intrigued me.

"You are looking for evidence of drug use — am I right?" He reached into his shirt pocket and handed me his business card.

Dale Abernathy, Chief of Police. It provided a phone number, a cell number, an e-mail address, and the physical address for the building in which I stood.

I unbuttoned my cuffs and rolled up the sleeves. "Chief, I haven't used drugs of any sort in over twenty years. And the little dope I used in my teens should be well out of my system." He held my arm as a phlebotomist would. He examined the soft skin on the inside of my elbow.

"Abernathy? That's the same last name as the owner of the Black Swan, Isaac."

"He's my great uncle." His answer that came without his looking up. "The captain's name is James Cobb."

"Thank you." I took possession of my arm again, rolled the sleeves down, and re-buttoned the large cuffs. "Are you always this odd?" He ignored me.

They were James Cobb and Samuel Selby, captain and mate of the schooner, Black Swan.

Sammy was the hallway bully, with his skinny, quiet buddy, Jimmy, standing next to him. Sammy was the street thug, Sammy, the mean mate with his dog, Jimmy.

I shuffled, pondered, and put a bit of spring in my step while I sauntered back to the vessel.

"Margaret. Did you have a nice walk?" I looked up to see the mate watch me climb down the companionway. "You went in the main entrance of the town hall and came out on the west side. Find anything interesting? What were ya doin' there?"

"That . . . would be my business, now, wouldn't it?" He turned his back to me.

Stopped halfway down the companionway, my eyes were level with the hatch. I looked down into the galley and focused on the hull number for the first time. It was a carved number, *6010861*, on a board. The numbers were painted in white with an infinitesimal black border scoring the outline of each number. The numbers were carved without ornamentation. This board sat below a brass plaque that read: *Lyttle Shipyard, Sturgis Cove, Maine, 1899, Hull Number:*

I descended, giving the numberboard a tap with both hands. Both arms over my head, I drummed the hull number with my fingers. It was a small act of defiance, a little bit of youth showing through.

Passengers boarded. I was surprised each time they arrived. Small patterns emerged during our trips. The processes of tacking, the rhythms of sailing, had started forming. The passengers' coming and going felt almost rhythmic. Our journeys among the islands and inlets of this region of Maine started feeling routine. I taught myself efficiency in my work: in my cleaning, in my cooking, and in my shopping.

The manager at the IGA agreed to freeze milk for me by the gallon. Frozen milk and my ten-pound blocks of ice kept the ice box cool for a week. Lettuce and tender vegetables would last only two days at sea. Frozen vegetables in bags would last the week, staying cold next to the ice blocks and the milk. I learned how to budget meat through the week so that none would go bad.

The mate and others disrupted these spells of success. I passively fought with them, remaining hidden in my galley. They'd wander bars at night when we were dockside. They'd run around in that truck, making crazy deliveries and being busy. I just let them run and be. If I put them from my mind, my bunk and my galley felt as if they belonged to me.

"Margaret. Margaret?" I don't sleep that heavily.

"Joe? What do you need?" It was full dark, well after midnight.

"David's hurt. Can you . . . ?"

I followed Joe ashore to a granite curb at the far end of the parking lot. "Joe, is he okay?"

"He's just banged up a bit." Both eyes were swollen, one nearly shut. Blood oozed from a couple of places on his face. A lip bled.

"David?"

He let his head fall back to see me. "David, answer me. Do you know where you are?"

"Yeah . . . . "

"We need to call 911."

I didn't want to adopt a couple of hopeless projects. "David, lie back, sweetie." I gave him a look-over, telling Joe to stay put and keep David still.

At my car, I dug my cell phone from the glove box. After the initial reports to the 911 dispatcher, I wanted to hang up. I wanted to walk back and check on the boys. I stood at my car as if the phone were tethered there. I talked while staring out over the dark waters. I put the words in my own mouth. "Sir, I'd like to hang up and check on David."

"We'd like to keep you on the line until the ambulance gets there. It will only be a minute or so."

I turned to walk back to the curb, keeping my cell phone at my ear.

"Joe? JOE?" I called out. "David?"

"Sir, they've disappeared. There were probably a little drunk too. I need to hang up and look for them."

I was just starting to hear a siren in the near distance.

"Joe?" I called and walked around, peeked around dark corners and small alleys that form between the brick buildings.

"Come on, Joe. I know you can hear me." The ambulance was now in the parking lot, splashing white and red lights spasmodically around the landscape.

“Sorry gents.” I addressed the two EMTs. “Two of the crew from the Black Swan. One is pretty badly beaten. They both sounded a little drunk.” They scanned the area with their eyes.

“We can wait a few minutes.”

“I don’t know. They clearly ran. I’ll look around.”

The two EMTs wandered with flashlights. Thirty minutes later, a policeman joined us. I found myself having to explain the situation and then myself to the cop.

“No, I don’t know them well.”

“No, I don’t know their last names.”

“No, I don’t know what bar they hang out in.”

“How long have I been aboard? A couple of weeks, I guess.”

The officer’s face revealed his incredulity. He asked if we all lived together on board. “Yes.” I explained the fo’c’sle and the galley as if they were a village apart. I described that they had a small head foreword and that I had one in the galley. “It’s a job. I don’t have to know them. It’s not like a slumber party.”

When asked who did the punching, I only had a guess. And that guess, I didn’t offer. There must have been a physical response to my thoughts, a look, an odor, or a twitch. I could see another wave of incredulity sweep over the cop’s face.

I yielded, sharing my suspicions with him. That brought us to a new course of questions, some of which we had already covered.

“Do you know the mate’s name?”

“Listen,” I said calmly, “my hunch is based on nothing.” Faced with a few tangible facts, I wasn’t ready to admit that I lived amongst these people.

“Do you know where the mate is from?”

"No."

"Is the mate on board?"

"I don't know."

"Is the captain on board?"

"Okay, sir. I just don't know. I haven't cared. And part of me just doesn't care that much. Calling 911 was simply the right thing to do"

"I want to look on your boat."

"Hah, my boat. You think that's my boat. I was asleep on that boat. As far as I can tell that boat and I are both miserable servants to a bunch of assholes." I walked away from him.

He grabbed my arm.

I turned with fury. "Sir —" I calmed, and the anger drained out of me. "You may either arrest me, which would allow you to touch me. Or you may release my arm." I stood tall.

I waited.

Fifteen years of training about workplace harassment, sexual harassment, and domestic battery, and I used them first against a police officer, in the middle of the night, alone. Nothing I had done was in the wrong. I could assert my innocence, for once.

We locked eyes. I cast mine down. I wished not to threaten him in any way. The scene dissolved quietly over the span of a few heartbeats. Just as good sense had prevailed over my anger, training and logic must have prevailed with the young officer as well. He released me.

I walked on.

He returned to his car, the EMTs, to their ambulance. The parking lot became dark and empty again.

The boys were in my galley. Joe stood over the firebox at the stove. There were cool, yellow flames coming out. He had just pushed a cardboard core from a roll of paper towels into the firebox.

"Here, sit down. I'll get it started." I offered. "Actually, Joe, lay David down so I can reach his head. Point his feet forward." Benches surrounded the table, hiding storage areas below and serving as bunks at night. A stair-step shaped affair with the storage spaces below the top bunk formed the backrest of the one below.

They both seemed drunk and stupid. Yet, I observed tenderness between them, one brother looking after another.

I filled a saucepan with fresh water, placing that directly onto the flames.

With a flashlight, I examined David. There wasn't much I could do, wasn't much I knew how to do. Wash and hope: first aid of the oldest sort.

David allowed me to clean him up while Joe rested on the bench near the mast in the middle of the boat. Never once did I hear a lament. Never did I hear the words, "why me?" I silently condemned the mate, Samuel Selby.

The fire in the stove mellowed and warmed us the rest of the night. I left the curtain open to my bunk and slept in my jeans. Both boys slept quietly in my galley. Their raspy breathing brought some comfort to me. It also exposed a twinge of loneliness.

"Margaret! You got my breakfast?" I had heard the mate's footfalls on the deck before he even approached the galley companionway. David still slept on the far side of the dining area. Joe was gone.

I took a position across the companionway, creating a physical barrier. He pushed me out of the way as if I weren't there at all.

"Come on, Saint Maggie, that stove been runnin' for hours. I've been seeing heat pour out of the charlie noble since dawn. You've got to have something ready to go, don' cha?"

I was unable to speak. All my cleverness vanished. So did the anger and my interest in accusing him. I didn't know what do to. *Can't show fear.*

"What's he doin' down here? David, get up. Time to worky, work-work. Get up boy."

When he started going toward David, I spoke, "Leave him be. You've done enough."

"He has to work. Davie, get up."

"Let him rest. You won, okay. Now, go away."

I had already been stepping back before the mate turned to face me. "Listen Margaret, this is my boat. You got that? Don't get in my way."

After he left, I ducked into the head. *Why should I shake? Why should I be afraid? He can't touch me. If he does, that will be a felony, a felony that will put any man away. That's it. No half-truths and no victim culpability. I'd sink him. He'd be gone.*

I started my shopping list and planning my menu. We had two paying customers for four days, four dinners, five lunches, and four breakfasts. We had a crew of four men: the captain, the fucking mate, David, Joe, and me. Thirteen meals for seven people, easy.

I still shook, sitting on my bed, waiting for the mate's steps to disappear off the Black Swan, leaving us both.

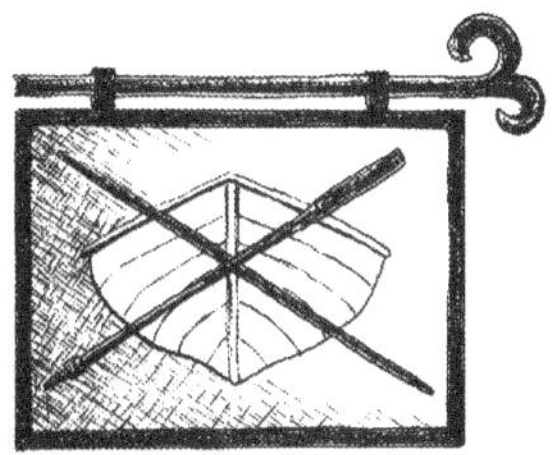

6. nunc *tempo: andante*

"BATS" is our crew's pet name for "Bar Across The Street." Others in town have called it "Ralph's Pretty Good Bar." Ask Ralph, a name he pronounces "Raif." He'll tell you the name of his bar is "Oar and Spar." Nobody cares what Raif calls his bar; the patrons call it what they will. To add to the confusion, the wood carving over the door looks far more like two baseball bats than a pair of nautical objects. We know that the carving is supposed to be oars or spars or both. That's the problem with the Red Sox winning the pennant: just about everything looks more like a bat than a spar. Poor Raif hung an image of two-crossed bats at his bar across the street. At least we strive to pronounce his name right, even if we refuse to spell it correctly.

"How are ya, Raif?" I call to him. Kieran offers a similarly hearty greeting. We are followed closely by Joe, David, Tad, Raven, (the black dog), and Stuart.

"Fresh off the boat, eh?"

Kieran accepts the barb, "What gives it away? The gentle aroma of the mother sea? The collective pungent reminders of Margaret's garlic potato soup?"

"No."

"Ah, the twinkle in our eyes that alerts the world to a new collection of stories?"

"No, not that either. You are loud, swaggering, dirty, and stinky."

"I believe, my dear, Raif, that I said all that in my very best Irish. Didn't I, lads?"

Joe and David have become quicker-witted in recent years, but still, neither can compete with Kieran for verbal boisterousness. David does struggle with something funny to add but regrettably, doesn't get it out fast enough. I see his shoulders rise and his chin come up.

"David," Tad turns to David. "Did Kieran break anything on my boat this trip?"

"I dunno, no, I guess. Not really." David, at the age of twenty-eight, speaks with the grace and confidence of a fourteen-year-old. He acts as if he is afraid of disappointing Tad, the new owner of Black Swan. He is afraid of ratting on Kieran. Thus he finds himself stuck.

Tad will keep trying to engage David.

"Joe, was it a good trip?" Tad addresses Joe, who is a few years older and now a foot taller than David.

When Joe starts his answer, we all lean in. I listen intensely. I hear "storm," "fun," "poem," and "good." He once just plain annoyed me. When he feels people are watching and listening, his voice softens. He can speak, just not at the moment he ought to. He's got a lovely tenor voice that he doesn't use. Joe is like a little boy, a stray. Both of these men are strays.

We so easily cast people from our midst without the little effort it takes to understand and to make room. Joe may have no place barking orders from the helm to a crew. He may not have a place in corporate meetings. Yet, and this is a lesson of the last three years, he does have a place. He and David have that element of humanity that I need to value. Saying that and living that are, at times, contradictory. There were times when ignoring Joe was easier than including Joe.

The former mate would ridicule the weaknesses in both of these boys, pick and pick at their scars and scabs. He'd hit them at their weakest. He'd hit them when he was drunk. I do blame the mate. But a goodly amount of the blame rested on Joe and on David for never having stood up to him—well, never but once, I guess. At any landfall, they would have been better to have wandered off the boat and into the byways of Maine. The blame rests on them because they'd return each evening after being ashore. They'd continue to return well past any justification I could understand. The IRS-reportable income was pretty horrible. The conditions were horrible. Their treatment was miserable. They never sought a higher authority. They didn't go to the police. They didn't talk to the owner. They returned for each trip, like strays with no place to call home.

Tad turns to Kieran, "Well, did you break anything?"

"Not this time, Gov. All is just fine. I brought the lovely lady home in great shape. She is as spry and frisky as a youth, y'know. I think she's getting better every day she's at sea."

I can see Stuart working his courage up to tell us all a story. He utters a word or two. He moves his shoulders closer to the middle of table. Then he finally catches the gap in conversation. "Once, when I was sailing on the Sloop Providence—"

Kieran stops him. "Now Stuart, darlin'. I've taught you how to start a sea story, haven't I?"

"Yes, Captain, you have."

"Well, then do it right."

"Okay, no shit, there I was, just minding my own business—"

"There you go. Now you can continue."

"—just minding my own business, when we got hit by this rogue wind. We were nearly close hauled and this gust came off our beam. We were flying the square topsail and every rag we could. That main had thirty-three thousand square feet of canvas. This wind comes. I'm on the windward side of the waist. The second mate's below me. One second, he's about to leap onto the steps to the quarterdeck. Instead, he's on his belly, sliding down to the green water below him. The wind put us over, almost flat, almost a full knockdown. The second mate's foot doesn't catch but goes right into the scupper hole.

"Now, this boat is a replica of the first ship in the US Navy. She is loaded with a four-pound cannon on the waist and one-pound swivel guns on the quarterdeck. I see the mate rolling aft, underneath number three cannon trucks. I don't think I even thought. I had fallen, but I caught on the hatch. I reached. I grabbed the bight of a line on the mast, swung across the vertical deck, and caught him by his outstretched hand. I threw him against the next cannon. We were already falling back to flat, so he smashes into the wood truck below cannon number two.

"The skipper is yelling for us to cut canvas. He is yelling at us for lying on the deck. He is yelling out of fear of losing his boat. And we are both bruised and trying to breath. The second mate, I can't even remember his name now, got the wind completely knocked out of him. He rolled and flew into that cannon. We both swung through green water that washed the deck.

"I totally saw him underneath old number three. I don't know how much those cannons weigh. Huge tubes of cast iron on massive wooden carriages. He would've been crushed dead. We both knew it. And we lay there — him suckin' for breath like he was kicked in the balls and me panicked still by the entire thought of it."

Kieran responds. "Bullshit."

Stuart is astounded by the word. Old insecurities come back to him. He goes mute.

Kieran sees it. "I know you, Stuart. You should have saved the second mate and dropped the main."

"The main is gaff rigged. I can't drop both halyards alone. Anyway, the skipper loosed the main sheet."

"You could have done it. All in a day's work, boy, all in a day's work. On my boat, I'd expect at least that." Stuart is recovering, comprehending that Kieran is kidding. Stuart looks at Kieran. He breathes. He stalls.

He tries, "You can do better?"

Kieran beams. I feel pleased.

"Of course. I was runnin' the streets of Belfast during my youth."

I jump in. "Runnin' from the streets of Belfast."

"Wanna go at it Miss Margaret? Are you going to cast a stone?"

I smile back. "Me, I am an innocent."

"That's what every one of your friends is saying to his lawyer now, isn't it? 'I am an innocent.' Meanwhile they're shredding documents before your S.E.C. calls on them."

"No shit, there I was just minding my own business when all of a sudden we found off-book transactions, lease-in/lease-out scams, and insider trading." I spar back at Kieran and put my arm around Stuart. "Well, I never did save a life. I am not a hero. Not like you."

"Me, I've never saved one. Why would you think I had?"

"For all your talk."

"Margaret, I am as full of it as you are, sweetie. Joe, have you ever saved a life?"

The table goes quiet. Each leans in.

Joe looks to his beer glass. His lips move. Tad looks to me. I look to David. Kieran looks to David. He'll come around.

Kieran jumps into the silence. When he has a beer in his hand, Kieran will leap into any silence. I drop my arm off of Stuart's shoulder. I want to be able to put my arm up on Tad's shoulder with the same degree of ease that I have with Stuart. Kieran makes us all laugh. I drift into thought about my husband.

My heart moves into my throat. I feel my palms sweat. I get scared. I breathe, focusing on the exhale. I exhale, again finding calm. Then, with an assumed casualness I don't own, I place my hand upon Tad's shoulder in a move no more intimate than the touch I offered David. I feel thrills when Tad relaxes.

Kieran heads into a well-known reprieve about the oppression of the Irish Catholic kid being kept down by the man. I feel Tad breathing a bit shallower. My own breathing changes in response.

I reach for my beer with my wrong hand.

I turn away from Tad. "Stuart, how did you get from that boat to this one?"

"I dunno, I wasn't a good fit there, I guess. I thought I liked it."

"David," I ask with a bold turn of direction. "Why didn't you ever leave Black Swan?"

"It's hard to leave. The money was good here, better before, y'know."

"It will never be like that again here."

"That's all right."

We have a regular table at BATS. It is round, in the corner, close to the bar, and away from the door. It has a window that allows us to view across the street, across the back lot and down the pier to our boat. Twilight cools the colors, yet her black hull presents strong geometric lines against the softer distant shores of the small island

and the irregular horizon. The Black Swan belongs at this coast, at this dock.

"Hey Raif," I holler a bit too loudly. "Can I have one of those monstrous cheeseburgers and home-cut fries?"

7. nunc *rondo*

Everything in this tidal world knows the rhythms of the moon. There are two clocks that rule this coastal life: the lunar clock and the solar clock. They beat syncopated rhythms.

With the twelve-foot tides, I follow the moon's clock at dock. I stock and clean while the boat rests at the height of the dock. We also try to board passengers at high tide.

"Welcome aboard, I am Margaret, the cook . . . "

"This is the galley—kitchen, as it were. Here is the galley head—bathroom. Your quarters are through this hatch. Follow on . . . "

"You may stow your gear here and get settled . . . "

Another group approaches.

"Welcome, I am the cook, Maggie. Francine and . . . Patricia? Welcome. Let me introduce Kieran, the captain. Then I'll take you below to your cabin."

"Dinner is on your own tonight. We'll have breakfast aboard at 7:30."

The food is all well stowed. There are fresh veggies and fresh meat: beef, chicken, pork. The vinegar bottle is well stocked with some new white wine. Linens are all washed: fresh tea towels, fresh napkins.

"Before folks leave for the night, let me show you how to use the head."

I worry more about plumbing problems than people getting hurt or tossed overboard.

"Behind here is a substantial first aid kit. I am an EMT, certified in the state of Maine. We've got a few articles for advanced lifesaving on board. I'd like each of you to find a moment to quietly review health issues and allergies with me before we get too far out to sea."

I count the folks in front of me, another full trip. I see eagerness and wonder. And awe.

"Good morning, I am your captain. My name is Kieran. You've met our cook, Maggie. Let me introduce you to our first mate, Stuart. This is his first year with us. Our crew: Joe and David. Joe is the tall, handsome one. David is the shorter, dark, handsome one." I wait a moment. Kieran smiles during his performance. Sometimes he tosses in extra lines such as, "Heck, we're all handsome on this boat." He'll read his audience and ad-lib.

"The main introduction this morning is not to us but to the ship we serve, the noble Black Swan. This vessel put to sea about a century ago on this coast. She's no teenager and requires a bit of our care. We're not one for having incidents, but we will be at sea, in an environment foreign to most of you and well away from help. Thus begins our safety lecture."

From basic orientation to the core vocabulary of sailing safely, to the duties, to life jackets, Kieran takes people through the essentials. He does it as if it were fresh to him. He tugs on PFDs, testing their tightness and fitness, allowing people to feel at ease and safe.

"The great powers of the sea captain have eroded over the century. I no longer have the right to lord over this boat and your lives as I may have once been able to do. I have tried, but people just complain. So I've had to stop. You folks are guests here to have a fun time at sea, and you are assuming some risk for having that fun at sea. I'll not yell at you, although I well may yell. I may speak bluntly. I may, in fact, give orders. Now, I can only give orders to my crew. But if you present yourself with skill, dexterity, and knowledge, please understand that if I do toss an order your way, it is a compliment. If you cannot follow through with an instruction—whether you feel unsafe, unsure, uncomfortable, or just get mad at me—you need to communicate that to me. You are here to have a good time. We are here to provide you a safe sailing environment. So just tell us what you are comfortable with and ask us for help. Can't get something done? Ask for help. See something you don't understand? Ask us. We've all chosen this path because it is fun.

"During moments such as docking, anchoring, storms, sailing evolutions, you'll notice we get a bit more serious. This is our office, as it were, and we'll respond to risk in the same way any professional does. So please understand this."

Kieran tends to let silence give weight to his statements.

"Now, I am the boss of the boat, but Margaret is the boss of the insides of this boat. She is the heart and stomach of the crew and the Black Swan. I may think myself the head. Pretty much, the world of living aboard is her domain: your food, comfort, health, and well-being. Maggie . . . "

"Good morning all. I am Margaret Noonan, your cook. I am also a licensed sea captain, a certified EMT, a native of Maine, and here because I chose to be. I have grown to love this life. There are a few basic rules for our survival on this boat. Just as the helm and the captain's quarters are Kieran's offices, the galley is both my office and my home. I cook, sleep, wash, pee, poop, and play in that small space down there. You are all welcome at anytime, just understand that unlike your staterooms, mine has no door. I'll know you are there. I'll hear you. Just be aware.

"As for the galley itself: I run an open galley. The food we have on board is all the food we have. We could live about a month if we ate canned goods and dry goods. But the fresh food is in the icebox and the freezer below it. The icebox is cooled, in fact, with ice, big blocks of ice and a few gallons of frozen milk. This is not your home fridge, nor your kitchen at home. There is a fine line between asking for food and helping yourself. I am here to serve, and I would often prefer to be asked if you need something from the galley. It isn't a bother to me.

"That said, I put the food that can be nibbled out in plain view. In the icebox, it is front and center. These are typically the leftovers. There's milk and fruit juice there, easy to reach. You cannot hang on the door and browse slowly. Open it; take what you need, and close the door. The ice doesn't last that long. And on that, please, please, please don't open the freezer. There is no ice cream hiding down there, no great hidden mystery. It is food preservation at the most fundamental.

"I move fruit from the icebox to the counters everyday. The bread that you find out is the bread I would prefer you nibble from.

"For the most part, dishes have to be used, washed, dried, and put away in a timeframe. I hate plastic dishes and drinking cups, so I have opted for glass and ceramic. The risk, of course, is breakage. Things break, I accept that. But if you take a glass from the cupboard, you can't leave it on the counter. Even with the thought, *Oh, I'll be back in a second.* Our little world is in constant motion. Use it, wash it, dry it, and replace it. If you must run, lay a glass on its side in the sink or tuck it between cushions. I hang metal mugs from a string of hooks. These are what I use for just about everything I drink during the day. Mine says *Maggie* on it. Each of the crew has a cup with a label. Take a pencil and mark one if you'd like. There are close to a dozen down there.

"For drinking on deck, I have Styrofoam cups. The metal mugs are best, but please don't bring glass stuff on deck. I have paper plates and paper towels if you want to bring food up here.

"I have covered all the noes and don'ts. This really is fun. We're just interested in keeping the food safe, you safe, glass and ceramic off the deck. We'd prefer to have you return home with fingers attached and heads un-banged.

"My menu is always flexible. I serve hearty New England-style food. It is plain and a celebration of the food itself. It is simple in that I don't have fancy equipment. I cook on a cast-iron stove that is heated with mineral spirits. It is what it is. I'll not get many soufflés or seared steaks from it. What I do get is roasted meats, breads, cakes, chowders, stews, and the like.

"We have learned to communicate with our guests prior to their arrival about the food. I know and understand kosher. I can't do kosher. I can't do sushi, sashimi, Thai, Laotian. I can barely cook Southern. I carry neither hominy nor grits. Chitlins, okra can't be found here. And I don't fry tomatoes; green or otherwise. Very little of my cooking involves deep frying. There is just too much risk of fire and spilling. So as long as you love what I serve, I'll take any complaint offered.

"Breakfast is casual. I will make what you want: eggs, pancakes, omelets, oatmeal. Heck, you can ask for eggs and a ham steak and get it. If you tell me the night before, I can make cornbread for breakfast. There is also an assortment of cereals. I'll put them out for the first days and see what people do. You are free to grab the cereal any time you'd like (given you wash the dish or give me the dish to wash).

"I make bread in the morning. Lunch is a bit of a hodge-podge affair: leftovers, sandwiches, soups. I normally have a lot of variety for lunch. Lunch is my opportunity to finish older meals. Meats go into sandwiches or soups, etcetera. There is normally fresh bread at lunch. I will occasionally do some fry-dough if the seas are calm. Fry-dough is also called Elephant Ears, Belly Button bread, and fry bread. I love mine with powdered sugar. I normally have jellies and apple butter on hand as well.

"I work slowly all day for the evening meal. It's normally well underway by the time I'm cleaning up from lunch.

"I love help. I am cleaning constantly during the day. I can always use a hand with dishes, washing counters, and stuff. The stove is a bitch to light. I normally do that around 4:30 in the morning. Then it remains on all day long. As a result, the galley is the warmest, driest, most comfortable place on the entire boat. Don't touch the stove. That's the warning you get. There are no knobs, no lights. It's just hot.

"A few rules about cleaning. First, is an odd bit about my sponges. I spent years battling sponges and their thieves. You can make fun of me about my sponges. I am tough enough to take it, but I do this for our health. First, a new clean sponge is used only for dishes. You can tell it is a dish sponge because it is fresh looking and has a nice consistent yellow color. When it is done being a dish sponge, it gets retired to a counter sponge. I cut one corner off."

I hold up a sponge with a corner off.

"This sponge is allowed to be used on food prep surfaces. I use them with bleachy water and soap, as needed. When I use a sponge to wash non-food prep surfaces, I cut another corner off."

I hold up a sponge with two corners off.

"This sponge can be used on cabinet fronts, shelves, and the like. I use 'em for cleaning spills and messes. They don't get used for stuff that touches food. When I cut a third corner off, they are out of my galley."

I hold up a sponge with three corners cut off.

"These are used on deck, for grimy, oily stuff, I don't care as long I don't see them near food or near my counters. You can wipe arsenic or petroleum products with them. If you need a new sponge for a grungy job, take the dirtiest sponge from the galley and cut it down. If you use a fresh dish sponge for a dirty job like cleaning a toilet, don't toss it back in my galley! Cut the corners off and change its function.

"Any questions about my silly sponge business?"

"Yes," says Kieran. We are about to drop into a practiced routine. With his natural Irish accent sharpened, he asks, "What do you call a sponge with all the corners cut off?"

"Well, laddie, here in the States, we call 'em contraceptives."

A few give us a token titter.

Kieran scans the passengers, "I think we're done with the serious stuff. Let's get this boat to open water. Why don't you folks arrange yourselves along the starboard side, a couple of folks per crew? Stuart, you'll take the helm."

I step aft of the helm. I'll watch our new mate, Stuart. Leaving the dock is normally a job that Kieran does or that I do. Kieran coaches crew and guests on their jobs while we prepare to untie from the dock and leave the harbor.

"Hello." One of the guests greets me in the galley.

"Hey there." I try to remember each guest's name, but I don't always get it.

"Do you need a bit of help?"

"Of course. Made bread before? Why don't you wash your hands and come around here?" I step back while he washes his hands. Two fifty-pound bins of unsifted flour rest on the sole, the beginning of bread dough sits in a large, metal bowl.

In glass jars, I have wheat germ, cracked wheat, and graham.

"Joe, all right?

"Yeah."

"Okay." Joe is on the early morning anchor watch. "Quiet?" He nods.

The guys normally get good sleep during the night, but Kieran likes to have someone up in the early morning. Dawn is hinting at its arrival with a gentle brightening of the eastern sky, a deep purple to the black that domes us. Days tend to end around nine. Joe and David have long made a habit of slipping forward to their bunks shortly after dinner is over, around eight.

I hear Kieran's head being pumped. Then I hear him brushing his teeth. I scan the horizon, trying to determine what sort of a day it might just be. I hear the engine room hatch open up.

I sit down on the aft companionway, waiting for Kieran to finish checking fluid levels and engine health. "Good morning."

"Good morning. Making your rounds?" he asks me.

"Yeup."

"Sky still up? Earth still spinning?"

"Yeup."

"Stove fired up?"

"Yeup."

"Are you well?"

"Yeup."

He asks all these as if we've just had the conversation for the first time. When, in fact, I make a routine of checking out the corners of my world with a regular circuit. I am ready to report to Kieran, my captain, that all is good with the world. The anchor is holding; the water is below us; the sky's above; people are well and safe. My stove is warming, and life is just plain good.

"Good morning!" I speak quietly to the first of our guests to enter the galley. "Coffee's ready. Cereal's on the table. Would you like a hot breakfast? Eggs? Porridge?"

I have a whole salmon thawing on the counter.

During story hour, the eventide moments spent telling stories by the helm, I scan the small group of passengers. They sit in a comfortable silence. Without an introduction, I begin telling a story:

"Once upon a time, not such a long time ago, on a vessel very like this one, worked a mate. This mate was a wicked man, an evil man. This mate, Sam Baties, as he was known to his mother and family, arrived to our village masked in the glamour of a person with a gentle nature. Old man Ezekiel sought a sailing master for his spry schooner. And with a handshake, Sam Baties became the mate.

"Locally, little was known of the man. His accent hinted a Massachusetts home. And yet, Ezekiel didn't seek references. He hadn't heard the singsong rhymes that followed Sam from town to town, from ship to shore. 'Sam Baties, the sailorman from Hades,' was one that children chanted. And from adult lips, rang this: 'There have been damned maties, mates of the damned, but none so damned as Sam Baties.' Sam Baties's legend followed him a month after he put to sea. Quick with his fist, quicker to flare, Sam Baties held his new schooner in an unyielding grip.

"To the village, it mattered little but that Baties bring a new profit to these poor shores. They said he may have learned his craft on the River Styx but drives a Coaster like no one's seen in a generation. Ol' man Scratch (as the Devil's known here-abouts) smiled broadly upon his bairn. Oh, people may have talked about the mate's use of a rope's end as a whip, but they didn't judge it too harshly. A little knotted device he carried in his pocket, a device he called his 'starter.' About the neck and shoulders, the crew would get a wallop if they slacked. What was this starter but an ancient tool oft used on ships at sea? There are none that say this life is an easy life. A life at sea: harder than most. The profit of the owners, the safety of the vessel at sea, the distribution of work through a crew of men, these be the charge of every mate. None doubted Sam Baties efficiencies.

"It was a youth, of course, that ended this reign and the false prosperity, a youth who becomes the hero of this tale. Sent by his uncle, this orphaned teen was instructed to share in the wealth and learn the ways of the coastal schooner. Trapped between a hateful crew and a home closed to him, our youth fought to resign himself to the darkness that now engulfed. None ashore wanted his acquaintance. They'll share the money and goods placed on the barrelhead, but they'll not countenance a flirtation with any so tainted by the mate. What goodwill the youth had sloughed as he boarded that black boat. In time, the boy could not look upon himself without seeing what the villagers saw in him. Like stories from ancient times, the character of this boy withered with each beating, with each criminal act, his soul shrank and shrank.

"And it was Sam Baties that ate that kind soul.

"Hiding behind a building during a rare day ashore, our lad devoured scraps from the trash of a nearby store. And it is there that our lad, with a hand outstretched, offers meat and marrow to one as hungry and lonely as himself. The black dog, at first skittish, learned to eat from the boy's hand. The boy accepted the licks and kisses from the dog. The boy sang Brandy Tree as he stroked the dog, a tune that hinted at hope and echoed old dreams.

"At sea, the boy's time was made easier with memories of his friend. Thought of the dog brought rare smiles to his face. During the next visit ashore, the two found each other. Again, they ate together and napped in a shady spot. At the close of the day, the black-haired dog had to be chided just so the boy could board the schooner alone. And in that parting, the lad exposed his re-grown soul. He bent and hugged that dog. The crew and the mate saw the dog lick our lad's face. Our lad rejoined the crew with the smile and hope he had shown his first day. The dog took to his haunches, sitting with patience and newfound trust.

"The mate immediately dispatched our hero to the worst possible work that could be found. Our lad was sent to scrub one of the many hidden holds, the most dreaded hold below the engine. This place was the single darkest, foulest, deepest place on the entire boat. It was a place so well hidden that no official could ever find it, aplace so small that only the smallest of people could sneak into it, a place so concealed that only the most precious of cargo would be placed there.

"The next day, the lad was sent to the chain locker. He was forced to purge the mate's fouled plumbing. For three days, our boy saw no daylight. It was only the mate's voice that he heard, a voice oddly calm, a voice that was almost kind, a voice that didn't reconcile with the blows our youth felt from the knotted rope.

"As the week ended, our youth believed his punishment concluded. During his isolation, he knew only when they were in harbors. The mate never allowed him on the deck during their times at dock or at anchor. When our lad rejoined his watch, he participated in both the loading of cargo and a few sailing evolutions. Most of the crew didn't speak to him, although they treated him gently when alone. On the return voyage, the mate pulled a small whistle from his pocket. With it, he played a gentle little tune, a tune the boy recognized as the song he sang to his loyal black dog, a melody so familiar to the lad that he had to fight from humming along, a song, now stolen from him, stolen and gone forever.

"The quiet youth screamed at the mate, 'Where did that whistle come from?' The mate smiled, smiled the smile of a victor, the smile a conqueror has when the condemned plea. As the boy charged the man, he saw that the whistle was made of a slender bone, a slightly crooked mammal bone, a thighbone of a mammal that stood about hip-high, a dog. Of a black dog? A black dog that didn't yet have a name to himself. A black dog that waited on the pier while our lad was tossed to the belly of the schooner.

"The boy crumbled on the deck. He cried in front of the mate. He wept and he sobbed. And he took most of the blame on himself.

How could he have allowed the mate to have seen the weakness of love? How could he have allowed that gentle black dog anywhere near this boat? How could he have allowed himself to smile or feel hope? These are the thoughts of our youth as he struggled to get up off the deck. As he got to his knees, the mate kicked him firmly in the stomach, then once in the head.

"The crew turned their backs to the mate and our boy. He lay there, unmoving, from the hours of twilight to moonrise. He awoke slowly with the mate at the helm and the deck empty of people. He dragged himself to the scuppers and slumped back into what appeared to be a renewed unconsciousness. Instead of sleeping, he drew his knife. And he thought. What was he to this mate? What did the mate expect? Did the mate expect a fight? No, he expected our lad to atone and return to the crew. He expected our lad to behave like a beast that has been beaten. He expected our lad to apologize for his actions. Slowly, he rose; awkwardly, he stood.

"With great tremors and weakness, with a head hung low, with great shame, our boy limped to the mate. In the instant between one breath and the next, our boy placed his knife between two ribs and into the hardened, sick heart of the mate. Open eyed and silent, the mate collapsed into our lad's waiting arms.

"He removed his knife. He took the mate's starter and the bone whistle. Then he pushed the body over the lee side.

"Three hours later, the relieving watch found our lad standing alone by the helm. That was midnight. At dawn, the mate didn't appear on deck. At 8:00 AM, the mate wasn't found in his quarters.

"Once on shore, the boy found a quiet place to bury the bone whistle, and he burned the starter.

> Someday, down by the brandy tree,
> I'll hear the Shepherd call for me;
> Call me to leave my happy ways
> And the shining world I know.

Sun on the hill, come go with me,
My days have all been free.
The pipes come laughing down the wind
And that's the way I go, that's the way for me."

Eyes were closed when I finished. I let people enjoy the still for a moment. Then I sang the boy's song from beginning.

"I go down to the brandy tree
Take my nose and my tail with me,
All for the world and the wind to see
And never come back no more.

Down in the meadowmarsh, deep and wide,
Tumble the tangle by my side,
All for the westing wind to run
And slide in the summer rain . . . "

"David, all right?

"Yeah."

"Quiet?" David has the early morning anchor watch. He nods.

I scan the horizon, trying to determine what sort of a day it might just be. I hear Kieran stirring below.

I sit down on the aft companionway, waiting for Kieran to finish. "Good morning."

"Good morning. Making your rounds?" he asks me.

"Yeup."

"Sky still up? Earth still spinning?"

"Yeup."

"Stove fired up?"

"Yeup."

"Are you well?"

"Yeup."

Life is good.

I'll make stew today.

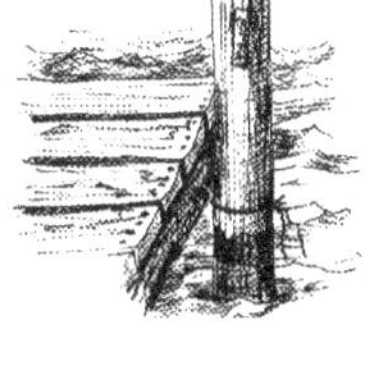

8. tunc *tempo: andante con affrettando*

Small routines appeared in my life. Passenger arrivals were spotty. The Black Swan must have operated at a loss. Customers would cancel. We'd drift out to sea with two paying people. We'd remain tied at the dock for a week at a time. I'd buy food for a trip, then have the trip cancelled. The mate would remove the meat and milk and eggs from the icebox for something he euphemistically called, "on-shore storage." Lettuce would be fresh, then brown, then tossed into the dumpster.

The routines appeared when passengers did join us: sailing during the days, anchoring at night. I'd make food during the day. People would awkwardly fumble through the evening with little to do. I put myself in the role of a steward. Through these days at sea, I peeked at elements of a good life. The mate was no kinder to David and Joe than he had been my first weeks. He was no kinder to me. We developed a sort of truce. For the first time since arriving at this shore, the mate seemed to be unsure around me. And I hadn't even used his name yet.

Our captain, James Cobb, was as invisible as ever. He'd present himself at the beginning of a cruise and pop out of his cabin a few times during the cruise. During the course of six weeks, I had prepared him a dozen meals. Frozen shrimp was his favorite. For breakfast, he'd eat oatmeal. He was a slender man. He wore black T-shirts, a trim black beard, and clean, black hair that was a bit wavy. He wore it a little longer than the fashion was in business.

When the Black Swan was at the dock, I was free to drive, explore, walk, and ponder. I adapted to this environment. It felt more like an extended vacation. And whether the Black Swan thrived as a business or not didn't matter one iota to me. I couldn't go back to the same position I had in Illinois. I didn't think the company would survive the scrutiny that must come. There would be investigations and allegations and charges. There would have to be. Officially, there had been some necessary reshuffling of personnel and divisions. In truth, I was offered a position during the shuffling, but it didn't carry the same heft. The title, when distilled down, read "special projects." I was being side-lined.

When it came to it, I was deeply hurt that they shuffled me. We were offering packages (a corporate term for layoffs with payoff) to scores of people, including management in my own division. I wasn't offered a package, but I moved from a position I had cultivated. I was being pulled from the front line.

I had a track record of delivering products and projects on time, on budget, and into a market that wanted what we had to offer. I never got beat in a battle. I never retreated, never surrendered. But no, we were eliminating divisions. They, these people who wanted to spin a great story for Wall Street and customers and investors, they wanted to be able to say, "We have new eyes on the case. Those heady days of off-books maneuvers are done, never happened."

You can't solve the same old problems with the same old solutions. But I didn't see any problems with my division that I wasn't aggressively solving. We were winning. Those were the rules we played with. If I am not making my numbers, then I expect to be gone. If I am making my numbers, I expect to thrive. I was making my numbers and growing my numbers and getting great projects and retaining great people, and, and, and. And that's it.

The guy who took my position, now his deals were always a bit hush-hush. He created a deal where his division sold fifty million dollars worth of services to another telecommunications company. He recognized that revenue to the books immediately. This revenue slid to the bottom line. He grew revenue, sure he did. Shiny-boy became a hero.

Just don't lift the hood and peek at the engine that drove his deals. It defied physics. He created a perpetual motion machine. This other telecommunications company was a former subsidiary of the same company to which we once belonged. We were parted siblings, as it were, competitors on the books, but once allies with still-strong ties. They were our customer, just as we were often their customers. Study their books, and you'll find that we purchased some fifty million dollars worth of goods and services from them.

They broke their revenue into a few divisions and quietly recognized it on their books over three fiscal quarters. My company entered into a leasing arrangement with them, "Company X," shall I call them? We paid this debt a little per month over several years. The lease was part of monthly operating expenditures — not even really defined as a debt. Who will miss some nine hundred thousand per month?

Of course, this all works out because Company X performed nearly a similar operation. They bought some fifty million in "product" from us. They leased it, breaking the payments into small, monthly bites. The trick is not to look at both organizations simultaneously. With so many transactions between two friendly rivals, these are easily missed in the volume of business between the two. Like finding specific grains of sand on a beach, the details are unrecognizable.

It's revenue that these companies count

Let's drive revenue. Let's show the Street a profit. Let's show growth. Give people a narrowly defined goal, and they will accomplish it within the established parameters. If that isn't a natural law explored by a great philosopher, it ought to be.

From a corporate perspective, if our funny behavior became well known, investors wouldn't trust us. But that is a future issue. Today's issue is profit. The trust can be earned again. If you doubt that trust can be earned again, look at Tylenol. Someone poisoned their product, and a decade later their brand is synonymous with over-the-counter pain relief. But we don't have to come to that point. These are just business deals, business deals that drive hard toward a favorable bottom line.

Profit is not an evil thing. Profit brings prosperity, health, education, and opportunity to life. I am a student of profit. At times, I am a priestess of profit. Capitalism has brought far greater stability and peace to this troubled world than any other economic or political system. It is not perfect, but it is the best that is available now. Never before had I been on the bad side of a decision based on profit.

I was profitable. My division was profitable. Our products and services were profitable. We sold and did what was asked of us. My failing was not looking to my flank. There was someone selling louder, driving more money to the bottom line, someone more charismatic, and someone they wanted in a leadership role. For the first time in my career, I was in the way.

In this little position they created for me, I was still to be a vice president. I would still be given the chance to compete and be promoted. So they said. They said, "We'll grow again, and we'll need leaders during that time." Imagine that, a reserve officer, as if that meant anything to me. You don't score points from the bench. People on the bench are not free agents. People on the bench sit on the bench. They are bench-sitting people. I do not belong on a bench. I belong in the game.

When the ego settled, I reassessed my situation. I had scads of money: stock, cash, bonds, and real estate. I had a C.V. rich with degrees from the right places and promotions at the right times: Oberlin and Kellogg School of Management. So I told Paul what I told the rest of the people: I had a new VP position with the same company, but I was going to take three months to sail and regroup before taking on the "exciting new challenges that my new job holds for me."

What a load of shit.

But it took lying on this rock, a rock I had named, The Flat Rock, to acknowledge my own hubris and to chuckle at myself while doing it.

So instead of being in an office on a campus of a telecommunications firm in Illinois in late June, I was in jeans too big to fit well, lying on a rock in the cool, dappled sunshine of a coastal Maine day. I was Huck Finn. I was a Barbary pirate.

I pulled up the bottom of my shirt to expose my belly to the sun. It wasn't warm, and I wouldn't tan. But I could be forty-four years old and show my belly. That was just the right reason for doing it.

Running sometimes doesn't get you anywhere.

I was on a wretched schooner, with a wretched, miserable, lonely crew. I was here, instead of being in a wretched office with a miserable, misplaced, confused staff, working with a company that was committing little bits of fraud. This view was certainly better.

Hours later, I walked back to the schooner. My feet were filthy. My shoes were in my hand. I had been walking barefoot as an extension of the Huck Finn attitude. I drummed on barrels when I passed them. I hit my thighs with my shoes. I whistled and hummed while I boarded the Black Swan.

"Hello, old girl." I tapped the railing while I came off the gangway. I dropped my shoes in the sun and went to swing down the companionway into my galley, a place so dark and sunless, it looked like a cave. No, maybe it looked more like a den, a lair. It was warm. There was food. It was my home. It wasn't a really horrible place. Instead of swinging down the companionway, I drummed with both hands on the hull number above my head.

It responded a musical hollowness. I tapped it again, giving a little rhythm to my effort. The sound was great.

But it didn't belong. I got curious. Why would a simple signboard be hollow? I gave it a wiggle, and it remained firm. I could see that the numberboard, which read *6010861*, had been fitted into place.

I drummed on it a few more times, then ducked below.

I still had half an afternoon to kill. With a freedom I hadn't had since I was thirteen years old, I pondered what adventure should be my next adventure. I lay on my bunk with my dirty feet propped up on the far wall, my hands under my head, and my elbows flailed to the sides. I decided that my dirty feet would look best if I rolled up my pants cuffs to mid-calf.

So I did.

Then I returned to the luxurious, reclined position. *Now what?* I asked myself. The answer came quickly. I decided to row. My grandfather taught me to row. I rowed with my father. In those days, few used motors in a boat's dinghy. I would take the wooden launch and row. I would explore the harbor alone. It was time to go see what could be found. But before rushing off, I lay there for a few more comfortable moments.

I grabbed an anorak, a Mae West, a bottle of water, a sandwich, and an apple. These, I put into a small backpack. Then I started the circuitous route to the launch. First, up the companionway to the deck, then off the boat to the dock, then down a ladder just aft of the Black Swan to the launch. I stepped in. And with the pedantic slowness of a student, I checked the boat: the fuel, the oars, the oarlocks, and the anchor. I tipped up the motor. I made sure that I was to be safe for my adventure. I untied, cast off, and took a few minutes to secure my oars in the oarlocks. I tried not to look as unpracticed as I felt.

I squared myself on the bench, centered myself in the boat. I started to row. Deep strokes. Shallow strokes. Uneven strokes that left a serpentine wake. With each flub, I focused on slowing down and doing it right. I hadn't rowed since leaving this coast in my youth, three decades before. Rowing was awkward, cumbersome and awkward.

I have learned to slow down when I discover myself acting clumsy. I put a little thought into each movement. I worked not to flail. Hurrying exposes the novice, whether in business or at sea. Nice, smooth, even strokes. People notice the smoothness. Speed, that comes with practice. *But even fast people go slowly,* I told myself. I adopted a casual, relaxed attitude on my face. I glanced about. When I paused, I studied something: a bird, a dock, a boat, or a movement. *Fake it until you make it, baby. Fake it until you make it.*

I crossed the open middle of the harbor. I came away from the dock with the boat moorage to my left and the opening to the channel to my right. My first destination was Flat Rock. From there, I thought I would row down the shore of the harbor, exploring the little inlet and beach just east of the rock. Then I would row out to Taft Point, to the causeway between the point and Taft Island. Taft Island sits just off the point. It helps close the harbor from the Gulf of Maine. The causeway is covered by water nearly one hundred percent of the time. Only during the extremely low spring tides do the barnacle-covered rocks expose themselves well enough to dry off.

For an hour, I rowed and drifted. I explored and rested. Floating over the causeway, which really ought to be renamed given that this bit of land is always submersed, I leaned over the gunnel to study the sunken rocks and their white, barnacled heads.

On Taft Island, I stepped out of my little boat to walk. I walked back toward the harbor to see two things at once: Black Swan not at her berth; Black Swan motoring down the channel toward the bay.

Standing in Teva sandals, one-hundred feet from my little boat and a long mile from Black Swan, I recognized that my home was leaving without me. My toothbrush was going to sea without me. My bunk, my clean clothes, my towels, my food, my car key were all going to sea without me. I did some mental arithmetic: time to run to boat, time to get rowboat to deeper water, time to start motor (with zero experience), time to reach Black Swan with outboard motor. All of this would require that I travel faster than she. And that became the obstacle around which I could not navigate. I had been left behind.

Even if I could travel faster than she, even if I did catch her, what would be the reaction of the crew? What would the mate say? How would the silent captain respond to having to stop the schooner to allow me to hop on board? Then what was the disposition of the launch? The launch was usually tied at the dock. We'd never put to sea with her in tow. There I stood, watching the Black Swan turn her profile away from me, presenting me with her transom. With her masts in a single line and her bows heading exactly away from me, I walked back to the launch. There was no urgency, but I desperately wanted to return to the dock.

It was a silly reaction. The dock was empty. There was nothing at the dock. There was nothing for me to do but sit at the empty dock, waiting for my toothbrush to sail back into view, for my bed to tie back up. I contemplated the existence of a note left by someone, explaining the boat's departure. I doubted one existed. I doubted anyone would have had the courtesy to write one. I disregarded the facts of my situation and directed my attention back to the dock. I pushed myself off the beach, rowing to deeper water. I then wrestled with the engine.

Pulling the engine from the water had been an easy operation when I was at the dock. I lifted it, and it automatically locked into place. Finding the release to lower the engine wasn't so easy. I had never been shown. I had never done it. I hadn't even seen the others do it. There certainly wasn't a sign: *Margaret, lift engine, press lever, lower engine.* I did find a lever and a process that worked. I lifted the motor again and let it lock into place. I then unlocked and lowered the engine. Another life skill I have adopted is to practice tasks when people aren't looking, then avoid embarrassment when people are looking. With another down and up and down, I certified myself as expert at lowering the outboard motor for the Black Swan's launch.

Starting the engine didn't come any easier. Luckily, the time I took to understand my stove lent itself directly to understanding a Yamaha outboard motor. The first dozen cranks yielded nothing but frustration. The little squeezes on the bulb I found on the gas line didn't help. Monkeying with the throttle didn't impact my performance. The engine wasn't starting, and no instruction manual existed on the boat. The ebb tide pushed me back toward the causeway, which brought little concern; it kept me from view and close to land.

My stove requires fuel, air (oxygen), and heat to work. An outboard motor, which operates on the internal combustion engine, would require the same key elements. If I wasn't getting a fire in the firebox (as I thought of the pistons and magic stuff inside the engine) then the failure had to be in oxygen, fuel, or spark. My first target became the fuel. It was most often the cause of my problems with the stove. Junk in the fuel line would cause me to open the fuel system and spill the mineral spirits on myself. I troubleshot that stove, starting with the fuel and fuel systems.

I picked up the gas can and shook it. It was full. At the origin of the gas line was a small valve. I turned it so it was parallel with the hose. This time, when I squeeze the bulb, it got firm, as if it had filled with fluid. I then turned the key from *On* to *Start* again. I actually expected it to come to life, but it didn't. I then thought about the throttle. I had to open the throttle to get the fuel to the engine. But, like the older Hondas I drove with a stick shift, I wondered if I needed to throttle while in neutral. There was a paddle of a sort that seemed associated with the throttle. I pressed this paddle and pushed the throttle forward, all the way. I turned from *On* to *Start* and the engine roared to life. It went quickly from a roar to a whine. I pulled the throttle back until it snapped into neutral again. The engine acted starved. I pushed the throttle forward. The engine sounded worse, but it started driving us through the water. I pulled back to neutral. I hit my little clutch-like paddle and eased the throttle forward again.

Success. With the engine at a comfortable idle, I thought, *Now it is warm enough to use.* I dropped into neutral again and eased the throttle forward. I literally puttered until I got a sense of the throttle, steering, and movement. I made a few circles, poured on a little speed, got nervous, backed off, and headed for the dock.

I wasn't ready to certify myself as an expert cox'n. I accepted "novice" for a few more days.

Given that I had never docked a powered launch, I thought I had done well, well enough to avoid damage and embarrassment. With grace, I lifted the engine to its rests, up and out of the water. Although, I hadn't found the engine positioned this way, I determined that this was probably the preferable means of stowage. It kept its appendages clear of the salt water. With a quick, practiced bowline cast high on the ladder, I secured the launch.

I climbed the ladder up to the dock. I looked about the parking lot and the backside of the village and thought, *This is what the dock looks like when we are at sea. This,* said I, *is a view I shouldn't see unless I had quit, been fired, or was heading home to Illinois.* The dock took on a different shape and a different meaning. The dock, with its big, square timber, was but a path to the Black Swan. *The timber is but a step, our doorstep. I am comfortable stepping off this dock.* Turning to look at the water, I recognized that my dock was no longer a step. Walk, step, and tumble. I had to tell myself, *Look, there is no boat there; don't walk off the dock.*

Of course, there was no note. I honestly didn't expect one. Neither did I find my toilet kit containing my toothbrush nor any such helpful stuff. There was no small overnight pack politely packed with clean underwear and a fresh T-shirt. Nor did I find my car key, my wallet, my purse, or any money. Because I am a woman of the modern world, I do have a habit of folding a couple of twenties around a single credit card and my driver's license. When my feet are on dry land, I always have this get-home-safe-kit at hand. Now, I had the kit and no home. My home sailed. It sailed off without me.

The practiced problem-solver in me identified options, assessed them, and worked toward a plan: food, water, bed, and some sense of when my stuff (and the boat carrying it) would be back. There certainly were a few restaurants and bars. During free evenings, I had poked around most of them, eaten in many. Bed? Now that presented a bit of a problem. During my first days, I drove many miles to get to a hotel. Without a car, the hotels I knew of were too far to reach. Inns? B&Bs? These had some possibility, given I had never inquired after them.

I walked into a bar called the Oar and Spar.

I took a seat at the quiet bar.

"What'll you have?"

"Do you have any iced tea?"

"Like brewed iced tea?"

"Yes, like brewed iced tea and not a Long Island iced tea."

"Okay, just wanted to be clear." The bar-keep paused a second. "No. I could make some, but that will take a while. Lemonade? I have some good stuff."

"Sure. As long as it isn't that cheesy drink-mix stuff."

"Nope, store-bought Paul Newman's Roadside Lemonade. I keep it here for myself."

Someone with a little taste. "Yes, that sounds perfect."

"I've seen you around a lot the last couple of months. New to town?"

"Yes, I am Margaret Noonan, cook off the Schooner Black Swan."

"Oh." His tone was a bit dispirited. Then he looked over my shoulder, out the dark windows. "Didn't she leave a bit ago?"

"Yes."

We both let the question sit there while he poured the lemonade. "Do you want a burger or something?"

"Something? Yes, I do. Got a menu?" He handed me one from the far side of the bar. I thought about the patrons, the turnover of the food, the state of his kitchens, and the organization of his refrigeration. I judged them all, sight-unseen. The burger was probably a frozen patty. A corned-beef sandwich on dark rye sounded great, if it was a great sandwich. Fish and chips both probably came from a box, poured almost directly into a fryer. That seemed the safest. It was a bar, after all. Bar food is a different class of food altogether. Bar food is designed to sell drinks. I pondered and sipped my extraordinarily good lemonade.

"Got a sandwich as good as this lemonade?" *Give the guy a chance.*

"Yes."

"I'll take it."

"Coming up."

Twenty minutes later, he returned with a po' boy on a bright pottery plate. Hand-cut potato fries were heaped next to it. The fries had skins on and varied in shape and size. The po' boy was well dressed with fresh lettuce, tomato, Creole mustard. It had sweet, spicy sausage and a hint of a thick, dark roux. The first bites were amazing. The fries had hints of vinegar and lemon juice, and the coarse sea salt was still visible. They were so fresh, and so good. I looked to him with praise, something akin to love and gratitude.

"My name is Raif." He introduced himself.

I smiled. No words could serve.

I may be homeless. I may be without a toothbrush, clean underwear, and a bed, but I am eating the greatest sandwich I have had in years. Umm. I took another pinch of fries and sipped from my refilled glass of lemonade.

He watched me eat. I hadn't eaten anything but bread for breakfast and an apple during my row. This food wasn't about hunger: it was about satisfaction. Like great sweaty, urgent sex after a long spell, like the comfort and warmth of your own bed after months of hotel rooms and airplanes, like the smell of my grandfather's woolen shirts and his sweet pipe tobacco, this sandwich slaked long-ignored needs. I didn't mind Ralph watching me; even that felt good. He watched with respect and some admiration. Each bite brought me pleasure.

With one half of the sandwich consumed, I placed it on my plate. I slowed my eating and took another sip of the lemonade.

"Wow." I blinked and nodded. I breathed and rested. "Do you know where the Black Swan went?"

"No." His "no" held something back, as if he'd said, "No, not really."

I gave him a studious look, one that said "bullshit" in a gentle manner. He had fed me a great sandwich. "I am somewhat stuck. I was out on the launch when she left."

"They do that once in a while."

"Do what?"

"Leave for a few hours or overnight. They are normally tied up by morning." He paused and then added, "They do this after a week or so of not having passengers." He said that as if I should know what he meant by that. "I've heard a few good things about your bread and your food."

"Really?"

"Yes, I have. Are you really making fresh bread everyday?"

"I try. I have been experimenting a bit. I want to get it down to one bowl, one pan, one spoon, and no mess. I'm close. I can get the dough made in minutes now. I measure nothing."

"Nice."

Given the size of the town and the fact we summarily dumped our passengers on the dock, it was no surprise that our passengers ended up in Ralph's bar.

"Are you liking the job?"

"I dunno." I answered more honestly than I had done with any passenger. "I can't imagine the experience matches what the guests are wanting." I deliberately used polite phrasing to probe his knowledge.

"Some are pleased with their time. The talk this month has been about you, I'll have to say. You seem to bring the light to the darkness that is that boat." Now that felt like a flirtation.

"I don't understand how the boat makes it. It can't pay its own way. I have spent my entire life in business, and this doesn't quite all fit together."

"Different motives, different needs, and not much overhead. Think of all the things that are missing: real estate, fuel costs, labor costs (you guys all work for close to nothing), costs of goods; none of that factors in. Old Man Abernathy is just happy to see his boat sailed. He doesn't care much. He's getting a bit soft, too. He must be past ninety."

"Humm . . . " I took more fries, still a little incredulous. Math is math; revenue is revenue, and expenses are expenses.

"Did Isaac interview you?"

"Isaac?"

"Did Old Man Abernathy interview you?"

"Over the phone."

"He does his hiring that way. And it is known. He rarely finds someone like you with his efforts. Why did you come here, anyway?"

"I wanted to."

He lowered his eyebrows in disapproval.

"I wanted to take a sabbatical from work. I wanted to come back to the coast of Maine, where I was born. I wanted to explore the world that belonged to my father and my grandfather and their fathers before them. They sailed here on schooners, fished and what-not."

"What did you do back there? Where is there?"

"Illinois. I am a vice president for a telecommunications company."

"Do I know the name?"

"I am certain you do."

"And they can survive without one of their young VPs?"

"I am changing jobs, going from one division to another during a reorganization. I thought I ought to take a break while I can."

He nodded. He understood more than I had credited him for. His food was far better than I had credited him for. The pieces of my story sorted and snapped into place while he thought.

"Any regrets?"

"Frankly, yes." *He is not a passenger. He may not yet be a friend, but he is the first person to ask a personal question of me since I got here.* The passengers had asked questions, but in every answer, I was selling the boat and trying to improve their experience, their comfort, and their sense of well-being.

He nodded.

"I am glad to have come here. But if the summer ended tomorrow, that would be okay too. I'm not ready to head home, but I am not sure that I picked the best place to hang my jeans. So, which are you? Cook, psychologist, or priest?"

"Oh, a bit of all of them, I guess. Bartender, I think."

"You didn't answer my question."

"Yes, I did." And he had.

"Okay, where did you come from?"

"New Paltz, New York."

"And your education?"

"College, liberal arts, English. Post graduate in forestry. Ski bum, smoke jumper, camp cook, suburban firefighter, cooked on a few schooners, including Black Swan, bar owner, volunteer firefighter, and town selectman. I sneak out to the Rockies and west coast to ski when I can . . . and the money for the bar came from early investments that I made in the 1980s with Microsoft and others."

" . . . which you sold in time . . . "

"Which I sold at the exact right time."

"Oh." I had never actually heard anyone say that.

"Yup. And I had some inheritance come in, and there was the family house that I sold."

"So all is good?"

"In fact, it is."

"Nice." Praise.

I had three reasons for coming into this bar. The first was to find food. The second was to get information on a place to sleep. The third was to determine why Black Swan had sailed out of the harbor on a quiet afternoon with no passengers and no cook on board. I hadn't learned the purpose of her departure, but I was developing confidence that she would appear before dawn. The food issues had been resolved. The bed issue was getting progressively sticky.

I had been drawn far enough into this conversation that I couldn't bring up beds, places to sleep, helplessness, or my current conundrums without further exposing a sub-text of our conversations. I was enjoying the flirtation. I was actually finding myself turned on by the attention, his warmth, his kindness, and his manner. And that forced the problem to be a bit worse than I wanted it to be. I didn't mind flirting or feeling this teenage quiver, but I wouldn't just go hop in the sack because I ate a great sandwich and was separated from Paul. Legally, I wasn't even separated. I'd explored the idea, but I hadn't come to the point of admitting it. I'd pulled the ring off at the Indiana border when I drove east. My finger didn't show the telltale paleness or indentations of a recently removed ring. My finger communicated a freedom I hadn't yet found in my heart.

Is it wrong to flirt and feel warm, stimulated, without the expectation of following through? Can't two adults flirt and play without the need to go further? With Ralph's intelligence, he could probably understand my situation, my temporary homelessness.

Dusk passed quickly, and the clock on the wall now showed eight. We continued talking, flirting, and exploring. I hadn't had a rich, full conversation in months. I hadn't had the joy of listening to an articulate person for a while. And I could say, pretty much, whatever was on my mind.

The conversation wandered, but we never strayed too far from ourselves. He'd serve a beer. He'd serve food and come back to me. At eight, I was on my second beer. My plates were gone. For the first time since Illinois, I found myself a part of something. Granted, it was a conversation with a man, but it was something.

With Black Swan gone, I missed my toothbrush, my underwear, and my car key. I missed a few things that make passing a night easier and cleaner. I didn't miss the damn boat or that horrible crew, a crew of which I was clearly not a member, a hateful, mean crew, an ignorant crew. I almost preferred to be a waitress in this bar than a cook on that boat, except I loved being outdoors, and sailing, and exploring, and the long quiet hours in my galley. I just hated the crew.

At eight-thirty, Dale, the police chief, entered the bar. He came and sat next to me. "Raif."

"Dale. Beer?"

"Yes."

"Alexander Keith's?"

"That sounds good. Maggie, what are you having?"

Ralph answered for me, "The same."

"It's good." I said to both of them. "How are you, Chief?"

"Fine. Your boat left you behind."

"Yes, it did."

"Good."

"Good?"

"Yes, good. Raif, you know this beer isn't legally for sale in this country."

"Humm, mighta heard that. Wanna give it back?"

"I'll just have you know, I am no Captain Louis Renault."

"Of course not, Chief."

"But I will have a second one. Maggie, my neighbor runs a B&B. I called her and asked if she had room for you tonight."

"Really, Chief? Isn't that just a bit presumptuous?"

“Might have been, but it was getting late.” And it was, but who was this man to take care of me? “I watched you playing on the dinghy this afternoon. I saw you tied up. My office overlooks the water from the second floor of the town hall.” He looked at Ralph, then at me. I didn't know if I wanted him to say anything or not. It was fun, but it wasn't public. “You don't have to take it, I was just trying to be nice. You are stuck, aren't you?”

“Yes, I admit it. I am stuck.”

He handed me a key and said, “Top of the stairs at the right. It has a brass plaque that has a number one on it. There are towels and toiletries in there for you.” I wasn't sure whether to take his actions as intrusive or caring. It would have been creepy if I didn't need them and if I wasn't in a village this small. And it did solve the problem with the flirtation, a flirtation that had quieted down with Dale's presence.

When I came down the stairs for breakfast, a pretty table was set for two. So I stood at the entrance to the dining room. There were about five empty tables and one that was set with dishes and utensils.

“Good morning. I'm Martha. Please come in and sit here.” She pointed to one of the two chairs at the set table.

“I'm Margaret Noonan. Thanks for taking me in last night. Sorry if I came in late.”

“Ten o'clock, that's not late. It's the folks that come in after midnight that bother me.” She spoke as if she knew me, and she probably did. Life in a B&B would be similar to living in a galley on a windjammer. “Good morning, Dale.”

He sat across from me and put the napkin on his lap. Martha poured coffee that she got from the sideboard. “French toast okay with you both?”

“Sure.” Dale answered for us both.

"You are presumptuous in the extreme, aren't you?"

"I may be, but she makes the best French toast I've ever had. You'll see." It irritated me that he neither missed my point nor chose to address it.

"I spent all evening with you."

"Yes. Well, you spent rather a lot of it with Raif. I think I was a bit of a spectator. Regardless, that was social. This is business."

The French toast did smell wonderful. So did the bacon.

"Business? Like police business?"

"Of course. I am not here to discuss the crooks at a phone company with you. And I don't think I can keep up with either you or Martha with respect to food. So, yes, police business."

"I take it my drug test came back negative?"

"Drug test? Oh, the hair sample. In fact it did. Yes." There was a boyish charm in this man. He had the energy of a twenty-year-old. His sandy hair was receding, and he had put on a bit of weight around the middle. *He works at keeping people off balance,* I thought.

"So, police business. Clearly, you are not interested in the illegal sale of Canadian beers?"

"Not much."

"And I haven't been speeding or stealing."

"That's right."

"So?"

"So, it's about the uncle's boat, the Black Swan."

"Oh."

"There's something wrong," he said, without much else. He wanted me to think about it. He wanted me to agree with him.

"Yes, yes, there is."

"Now, I don't know what it is. This is the coast of Maine. You can almost spit to Canada in two directions. This state borders Nova Scotia, New Brunswick, and Quebec. And in the Saint Lawrence Seaway sit two little islands that still belong to the French, a little enclave of Europe in our midst. People have been trying to make a living off of this coast with boats on the sea for hundreds of years. We've tried fishing, timber, granite, manufacturing, and nothing, nothing has ever paid what smuggling has paid. And that's the short of it."

"You are wondering if the Black Swan is smuggling?"

"Yes, I am."

"And you want me to help you find out?"

"Yes, I do."

"You want me to spy for you?"

"Yes."

"Why?"

"Because you haven't participated in the past."

What an arrogant shit! I felt as if he had insulted me. I still had my car, money, and everything I needed to stay free of these problems.

He continued. "Look at the market around us. Look at the news that's starting to break, and look where you are. For one reason or another, you don't seem to be standing in the field of play as the stories about Enron and WorldCom are poking up in the news. You're here, playing cook and nursemaid to a crew of boys. You were not on board when the crew took the Black Swan to sea last night. When the real trouble starts, you seem to be somewhere else."

How could being told that I was a decent, law-abiding person hurt? I could not pound my fist down, rattling our breakfast dishes, exclaiming, "I have perfect situational awareness." I could not say, "I know what's going on around me." It simply would not be true. I was standing in a glass box, thinking I was hidden. I was thinking I was in the game when, in fact, I got benched when the game started. For all my education, degrees, training, certifications, and all, I had not seen that I occasionally got special treatment, occasionally. Not always. I have certainly gotten rough and tumble. I have enjoyed that too. Have they thought I wasn't tough enough to handle it? Too good to be tainted? Was I some saint they wished to protect? Is this some ancient, gender thing, some form of gallantry? I hated having the gender-thing tossed back at me, but I wouldn't show it.

With a smile and a spin on my thoughts, I said, "Listen, that crew left me behind because I am new. They don't trust me."

"That's right." He took a bite of his French toast, a bite covered with homemade strawberry jam. "You seem to have the good luck to be away when there's trouble."

I must have revealed something in my eyes or my body language because after another bite he said, "I don't know anything more than that. You could be a huge embezzler. You could be involved with significant insider trading. You could be channeling massive amounts of cash to off-shore banks. I don't know that. You could be one badass babe, running from the law, hiding on my uncle's boat. That sort of thing has happened in the past."

I absorbed that. He said it with kindness too. He meant to be kind, and I was bristling at his every word. Neither did I want him to think me a crook, nor a saint.

"You don't have to answer me. This is nothing official. If something is going on, I'd like to know. I'd like to know before the US Coast Guard, US Customs, ATF, DEA or some other agency of the Federal Government stomps around and seizes every asset my family has built in the last one-hundred and fifty years."

"I don't know what to say."

"I do."

"Of course you do. You seem to like making decisions for me."

"Have I been wrong yet?"

"Presumptuous. Arrogant."

"But wrong?"

"Okay, not wrong. You have it. You are an arrogant, quirky cop."

"That's right." He got up and left.

I stood to walk into the kitchen, but Martha met me at the swinging door. I handed her my credit card.

"Not needed. Dale paid for it."

Bastard.

I saw the masts of the Black Swan above the downtown buildings and houses that were between Martha's place and the harbor.

9. nunc

tempo: allegretto con grazia

Damn!

Damn, damn, damn.

I feel a case of the weepies coming on. Coming on? They are here. Little thoughts cause disproportional responses. I am weeping again. Not a real cry, just a baseline sadness that keeps a tear at the outside corners of my eyeballs. I wrestle with doubt. Little questions become big, unsolvable problems. Should I make stew or chowder? Which do people want? Which do I want? What would be better? How do I make this decision? Why do I have to make this decision?

I have come to view these little crises of confidence, these episodes of sadness and doubt, as akin to colds. They come. They go. I feel them hitting me harder on the boat than I did back in Illinois. I had them then too, but I would push through the day and dump everything on Paul. He came to recognize them. He'd take care of me. He'd make meals for a couple of days. He'd rent the movies. He'd pick something fun to do on the weekends. He'd clean up. As if some meter in my body displayed, "full" or "empty" (for I never know which). Sometimes, it is a great emptiness; sometimes, it is a sense of overload.

Stupid issues could stall me: shower or bath, get up or don't get up, what's for dinner, or what to wear. Each of these decisions would take on weight that was unwarranted. I would begin to examine the depth of the decision, its impact on the greater context: long term, short-term, financial, resources, etcetera. My mind was so practiced at making decisions in a professional environment that an internal debate between a shower and a bath hit with the impact of a spanner tossed among a series of happily spinning cogs. The engines of my mind would grind.

In the corporate world, I would show a little tiredness and a little impatience. That long ago life and its decisions were practiced. It allowed me to get through an episode in a couple of days or a week. I'd remind myself to delegate more. I would practice patience when folks reviewed their own doubts and thoughts with me. In a week's time, this would all pass. If it didn't, I'd find a way of stepping out of the office for a couple of days. I would change my routines and just break the cycles.

This particular life doesn't allow for that. The cycles simply exist. If the stove isn't lit by 4:30 or 5 AM, then there is no hot coffee, no hot breakfast, and no hot water for hygiene.

Before leaving Illinois , there had always been Paul. He was there. I could go home to him if I needed to. The longer I am here, the further I am from family, from home.

I have this freedom, this amazing freedom, freedom the size of the universe. I have no ties to anyone or anything, no little bits of string pulling me back, no lines connecting me to anything. I am definitely not an ill-defined, scribble-person with messy boundaries and messy lines connecting me to everything all over the place. Nothing's pulling or dragging on me.

I don't have to explain anything to my mother.

I don't have to wonder about Paul's reactions or what I may be doing to our relationship.

I can have sex if I want to.

I can buy a gun.

I can live in Europe.

I could have sex with another woman, with two men at once.

I could bleach my hair.

I could get a boob job.

I could bleach my hair, have sex with men, women, and my new boobs, all while trying some exotic designer drug.

I could do just about anything I wanted.

And here I stand at my cast-iron stove, alone, in the cavernous belly of a hundred-year-old schooner on the damp, cool, coast of Maine, thinking I don't want any of these choices.

After forty years of living in houses. I am homeless. I am without a home. I don't own a home. I have the money and the financial incentive to buy one, and I don't want one. I have been renting one for a couple of years, but that doesn't count. It is as much like camping as living on Black Swan is. It is barren.

Was getting the divorce a mistake?

Was signing the papers a mistake?

Damn!

What is to keep my feet on this earth? What will prevent me from just drifting away?

If I did buy a home, where should it be?

Why couldn't I have run all the way to Côte d'Azur? Florence doesn't have this raw coolness.

With Stuart, the new mate, stepping onto the companionway, I take a towel, wipe my face, and put a fresh strawberry in my mouth. I'd rather him think he caught me eating.

10. tunc *tempo: allegro vivo*

"Welcome back, Maggie. We missed you. We got wicked hungry without you." The mate found me in the galley.

"You lived."

"We had to go practice man-overboard drills and fire drills. It's a Coast Guard requirement."

"Oh. Okay." I didn't care if he lied to me. It didn't matter one bit to me. "I had a nice night ashore."

"You didn't do anything I wouldn't do, now did ya?"

"I haven't any idea about what you would or wouldn't do."

"No reason to be like that. We just went down the road a bit, banged a left, and did what the Coast Guard tells us we have to do."

"That's fine."

"I just thought you'd want to know."

"Okay. You went out and practiced safety maneuvers as required by law. I got it."

"That's right."

He couldn't figure out how to the end the conversation. I don't know what he was expecting. I treated him with the same contempt and coldness I'd treated him every other day of the week.

"We got people comin' tomorrow. Four and a kid."

"Okay, I'll get things ready. How many days are we going out for?"

"Four."

You can go now, I thought. But my thoughts didn't impact his actions — never had.

He asked, "You got any coffee?"

"No. Stove's not lit."

"All right, I gotta get a cup a coffee."

Even his voice grated on me. He had this nasally accent. Words were clipped, Rs dropped helter-skelter (helta-skeltah). Just about everything this man did, said, or thought irritated me.

With him gone from my galley, I relaxed. I pondered my other adventures. I decided to return to my exploration of the hull number: 6010861. I partially climbed my companionway. I turned, resting my backside on the ladder. I tapped the numberboard again. It was definitely hollow. And the numberboard was definitely a separate board, snug, but with just a bit of play, with focused study, I could hear and feel its laxity.

From the bottom, looking up, you could see that the signboard was an insert. The board showed clearly. There was a black line, a tiny gap between the backside of the signboard and the ceiling overhead. On the starboard side, on the bottom, there was a small hole, ringed in brass.

I stepped down into my galley and got a small, crappy kitchen knife and a small screwdriver. I confirmed the gap by running the knife behind the sign. I then put the screwdriver in the hole. The screwdriver didn't go in very far, but I did sense a spring or something in there. I pushed up, but the screwdriver simply went to its maximum depth, nothing but a few millimeters. I then wiggled, left, right, inboard, and outboard. The board had a bit of freedom. I leaned and pushed the screwdriver outboard, starboard. I pushed the board sideways as if to drive it into the deck. It moved about three-quarters of an inch — not willingly. I pushed harder. The board went so far, then stopped. When I released my pressure, the sign returned to its home.

I moved the board a few times, not in an effort to release it but to discover its movements, to help me think, and to help it get free. Then I saw it. I pushed it sideways and pulled it toward me. Actually, I had to pop it toward me with the knife. The board came out an inch or so. It rested a bit cockeyed. One push, wiggle, and pop, and it was free.

There was a significant space concealed, some four inches high, twelve-to-fourteen inches wide, and deeper than my arm could go. It was just a plain little hidey-hole. I guess I wasn't too surprised—just a bit of confirmation of the guesses and rumors that, in her ancient, smuggling past, this old schooner had run with a rough crowd.

When I went to put the signboard back in, I noticed that it was symmetrical. It could go in with the numbers reading:

6010861

or

1980109.

Now I was a bit confused but not necessarily about the purpose of the ruse. Clearly, someone wanted to be able to change the identity of the Black Swan, change it easily and quickly. My confusion rested on which was correct. Which end was up?

We couldn't have hull numbers that didn't match the documentation. Coasties would get a bit annoyed at that. Couldn't set it right while they watched either. I tried the board one way, then the other, holding it at arm's-length.

I examined dust, dirt, grease, and wear marks to give me a clue. It had spent a great deal of the century being moved about, but the dirt lines from the last decade had left a bit of an impression. I seated it back into place: 6010861.

I did find a nice, concealed, dry storage space, if I ever needed one.

"Welcome aboard. I am Margaret Noonan, cook. Welcome aboard the Schooner Black Swan." Names were offered, hands shaken. All five arrived at the same moment. I had watched Joe greet passengers the last time. It set people back. They could not understand him. The mate regarded the job with utter contempt. And that captain never moved from his cabin one day to the next. David did well, yet if David saw me at the rail, he retreated to the fo'c'sle.

During recent weeks, I'd developed a checklist of items to review with passengers when they boarded. I carried a clipboard with these items written on them: quarters, lee cloths, head functions, galley, hours, and duties. I gave them a short tour of the boat.

My vocabulary and understanding of the operation of the Black Swan had increased in the two months I'd been aboard. I could, with authority, lay my hands on the main throat halyard, the main peak halyard, the fore peak halyard, the fore throat halyard, the jib, jumbo, and flying jib halyards. I could identify each line on the starboard and port forward pin rails: jib sheet, jumbo sheet, flying jib sheet, and cat for anchor. The few lines I didn't know, I left out of my tour.

I described duty stations during evolutions such as hoisting, tacking, waring (gybing), docking, and anchoring. I was a regular salt. The five people listened with polite attention. *Maybe,* I thought, *some already have this knowledge.*

By 4 PM, I bid them adieu until breakfast at 7:30 AM, *zero seven thirty*. I sent them off to town with a strong recommendation for the Oar and Spar, a place I now called a tavern. "Try the Alexander Keith, you can't get that in most places," I told them.

Since my evening with Ralph, I had made strides to improve the quality of the food in my galley. I wanted to make more from scratch and rely less on prepared foods, mixes, and the like. It was a recognition of the challenges, a recognition that I rose to challenges.

During my tour, I pondered the hull number trick again. Changing the hull number wouldn't do any good unless one could also change the vessel name. I surmised that the name boards on the bows and across the stern would each be removable without the use of big tools. Changing names would have been done quickly, easily, in the dark, and while underway if this ruse were to work.

With this hypothesis in mind, I took another circle tour of the deck. The name on the bows was carved on wooden name boards. The steel hull had a brace designed just to hold them. There was a clever mechanical sliding mechanism that also used springs to secure the name to the hull. The ornamentation all remained. Just the name was removed.

She could be "Black Swan" one day in one port and "Martha Washington" or "Liberty" or something else an hour later, hum?

None of this could be news to the Abernathy family. Certainly, they had owned this schooner for decades. They would have known her history when they bought her. Or maybe they had her built? Maybe the Abernathys and their one-hundred and fifty years worth of fortunes included smuggling. It is often said that all great fortunes have roots in crime.

There must be other hidey-holes tucked in and around the hull of this boat.

Thus primed, I started my adventures in the late afternoon. I used the handle of a small screwdriver to find hollow sounds. I used wits, the business end of the screwdriver, and a knife to expose the little niches, little hidden spaces. There was almost a boat within a boat, so many of the cubbies had hidden compartments below, behind, and above.

The evidence of the transition from cargo transport to passenger-toting schooner was clear as well. The cabins were built in what appeared to be a former center hold. This center hold took almost one-third to one-half of the entire length of the boat. Throughout this newer construction, which included the passenger staterooms and heads, there were no hidden secrets. But my galley was full of them.

Some places where I expected to find them, I didn't. Under mattresses and other obvious places, I found just what I expected to find: well-planned, easy to use and find stowage.

Here she was, an infant born of the Victorian Age who, under her skirts, plied a hidden trade. She sailed these waters with great white sails and a black hull in full view of the fast and powerful revenue boats. Speed was a gift to her, but she could never compete against a powerboat in a race. The wind was free and sailing nearly silent. Her anachronistic technology gave stealth in the twentieth century.

But I couldn't believe that her income was derived from the cubic yards of space that I found. There had to be times when her entire hold was filled with contraband material. I was guessing, of course. These niches were probably supplemental to her primary efforts. My imagination ran to diamonds, rubies, gold, illicit drugs, secret documents, bearer bonds, cash, articles of high value requiring small volume for storage. Maybe she ran this coast with the purchased cooperation of a few officials, or maybe she paid a few debts with liquor from her hold. Maybe she had spent a lifetime doing sleight of hand tricks. Maybe her crew and owners hid the real illegal activity below a veneer of less illegal activity, concealed by posing as a coastal trading schooner. Oh, the possibilities were fun to imagine.

I'd heard passengers give a mighty "argh, matie" and an occasional not-so-salty "ahoy there". These passengers let their imaginations play, envisioning themselves on a pirate ship. I started to think that they had a part of their vision correct. The noble Black Swan may not have been a pirate ship in the most traditional sense, but she had clearly been engaged in extralegal activities.

Three days later, our small crew and five passengers were anchoring off Rodel Point, one more night out before heading to the harbor. We dropped the hook about an hour before sundown. The land radiated warmth over the cool water. I turned west-southwest to find the fading heat of the sun. Two seals played on the rocks about a half-mile distant. I believe I expected to see the orange mooring buoy, for seeing it didn't seem out of place this time. We had anchored close enough to it so that the buoy rested on our hull. Joe and David were securing the fore boom into its crutch.

I walked to the rail and looked down on the buoy.

I felt little stabs of anxiety when I heard movement on deck. As I heard the aft companionway open, I stiffened. I turned my gaze to the seals. I instructed my body to relax. I told myself to breath comfortably. I was safe. I was entitled to this spot. I was not a dog to be kicked and shooed away. There was nothing here I shouldn't be seeing.

"Saint Margaret." The mate approached me. "How's dinnah comin'? Enjoyin' yourself?" He came right next to me. "Watchin' them two seal get it on are ya?"

"You know, Sammy, you really are a fucking pig." With that, I walked away.

"David," I heard the mate call out in a hushed tone, "Come 'ere boy! Make this fast."

I chuckled while I walked toward the galley companionway. He wanted to chase me away.

I watched Joe and David hook and haul the buoy on deck, tie a line to it, and drop the orange ball over the side again. They tied it all off forward, near the anchor. I gave the hull number a tap when I ducked down into my galley: onions, garlic, caraway, fresh bread, and moist warm aromatic air. I picked out hints of the bilge and some bleach odors. It had begun to smell like a home.

After all the dishes had been done, after passengers stopped whispering in their staterooms and had fallen off to sleep, after the teenage boy (odd number five of our guests) started snoring on the far side of the galley, I lay, waiting in a gentle, light sleep. When I heard the mate step to the deck, I looked at the watch I kept on the wee shelf near my head: a bit after midnight, 12:30.

I followed the activity with my ears: mate walking forward to the fo'c'sle; three pair of feet; Joe, David, and the mate returning to the quarterdeck; and the metal-on-metal sound of the boat-gaff hitting the hull. I had heard enough to understand they were hoisting something on board, something that had been attached to the orange mooring buoy. I drifted to sleep before they finished. It became clear to me that in this current age, the buoy was a rendezvous point for hidden cargo.

I spent the morning cleaning my galley and preparing it for my days ashore. I made omelets with leftover pork, onions, peppers, and some cream. For lunch, I prepared the table with slices of beef, a cold chicken leg, a bit of tuna fish from a can mixed with the last of a small jar of mayonnaise. I took the remains of the salad fixings and tossed them about with some dressing. Without refrigeration, nothing keeps while we are at the dock. Everything open or perishable must get eaten or get tossed.

After our casual lunch, I scraped the remains into the slop bucket. My galley companion, Number Five, as I came to think of him, emptied the contents of our bucket over the side for the fish, the seals, and the birds to enjoy.

We had been doing this enough that I was able to time things well. I washed my counters with the bleachy water. I washed the sole with a mop. I was wiping my hands on a towel when we started the right-hand turn into the harbor. I came on deck in time to help lower the foresail while we entered the harbor.

The captain, James Cobb, made an unusual appearance on deck. He stood at the mate's left shoulder while the mate guided the schooner toward the dock. We navigated through the harbor on diesel. The mate laid us alongside the dock with an expertise that brought me some pride. Our bows were pointing toward the harbor mouth, our stern toward the shallows. Joe, David, and the quiet, teenage Number Five dressed the port side, ready to make us fast.

And there, following our bows, with his arms outstretched, ready to catch a line, was my husband, Paul.

11. *nunc* — *tempo: vivace*

When June draws to an end, the moon grows larger. I develop a sense of swelling, a great need to burst. July just wants to explode.

Tides are bigger, currents stronger, bodies more exposed, evenings longer, and nights, warmer.

An ancient Irish, ancient pagan spirit grows unrepressed within me.

It is time to dance, time for a great fire, time to drink.

There is even a little something inside of me that says, *Time to breed* — not just sex —time to make the belly swell, to engorge on the bounties that surround us.

I spend one afternoon and evening digging a hole on the beach. We put to shore for a two-day break, and I start by digging a hole I can stand in, a hole in a rocky, gravelly beach. I scrounge old tarps and old sails. I stack driftwood and building scraps. I steal firewood from Dale Abernathy's back yard. I steal it by the wheelbarrow-full. I sleep. I wake.

I fill the hole with fire, then big rocks that shatter logs when they fall, rocks that toss red sparks. I make a salad of rocks, fire, and logs.

Before dawn, I have a white-hot fire burning in that pit.

I lie on the folded tarps and the old sails. Dawn explodes overhead: golden-trimmed clouds, pink clouds, purple skies, and fading stars.

I haven't planned. I haven't discussed. It is just time for this, and I know everyone knows it too.

The sun is proud of the horizon, and I go to shop: lobsters from friends I've made over the years. I tell them of a party so great they promise to end their days early. They give me pounds of clams and pounds of mussels. What I can't beg, I buy.

I dance through the grocery store: butter by the armloads, corn from wooden crates, and two boxes of kosher salt.

In town, I tell David and Joe to bring seaweed to the fire pit.

"Feed it wood. Keep it hot."

I beg Ralph to call his friends. "Get the fiddlers! We need men on drums. Men beating the bodhran."

With Dale's wheelbarrow full of corn and butter and salt, I push it to the beach.

"More rock!"

I am a woman afire.

I drag folding cloth chairs and old plywood near.

Rocks explode in the heat, tossing shards harmlessly into the walls of the pit. The air shimmers with escaping heat.

The day warms. I get hot. I drip with sweat when I push little David into the harbor from the dock. He bleats when he hits the water. I can only laugh.

I land with my mouth open. Water fills my cheeks and storms up my nose.

Joe stands there above me, having pushed me in. I give him the finger, laughing on. I slip out of my jeans, pull off my T-shirt, and hang them on the launch. I swim the length of the Black Swan, braced by the cold. Then, I swim back

Like an atom in an H-bomb, I bounce off everything that moves. I drive my energy into them all. They start bouncing off each other. I chase Kieran with a bucket of seawater. I stop abruptly when I see Tad. It is on him that I dump it. Then I steal his beer, drink half, and give it back to him.

Two dinghies are now on the beach. People gather. People drink. A pickup truck parks on the green lawns above the beach. Raven, the black dog, chases a playful child.

Lugh crosses his zenith. Dale, now in shorts, uses his wheelbarrow to gather seaweed.

He kisses me.

A crowd gathers while he lays layers of seaweed on the salad of hot rocks and red embers. A great steam rushes skyward.

People join in, tossing seaweed.

A group of four carries a blanket full of potatoes from a nearby truck. The group pours the potatoes into the steaming seaweed. A shopping bag of onions joins the potatoes.

No one needs to be told what to do: stone soup.

Another layer of seaweed.

Many hands toss scores and scores of lobsters and more seaweed.

We tie mussels in brightly colored sheets. Clams bake and steam, wrapped in red fire trucks and faded blue clouds.

A layer of sea-soaked corn. More seaweed.

My pit is full; revelers cover it with the sails I scrounged. We cover those with a few rocks.

Tad and his cousin, Dale, wheel an ancient Weber barbeque down from the great house. Someone produces a huge pot; others peel butter from paper wrappers and start coals.

When the fiddlers appear, most of us move up, off the beach. I am the first to dance.

Afternoon wanes. I grab Kieran. I give him a great kiss on the lips, both hands on his cheeks. The crowd cheers, and I pull him after me.

They play jigs, reels, hornpipes. Someone calls a few squares. Cloggers do a bit on some plywood. Beer bottles overflow the ad-hoc collection spots. Teenage girls pull guys into the dancing circle. The grass goes flat and brown beneath our feet.

At sunset, four men present a sheet of corrugated metal to the middle of the circle. Boys, women, girls, and a dog follow with sticks and wood. With a splash of gasoline and a tossed ball of burning paper, the pile erupts, roars. Dancing continues.

Sparks become visible; darkness envelops.

In gloaming, Dale announces that food is ready. A Costco-sized case of paper towels rests on folding tables on the beach. Stacks of paper plates and boxes of plastic utensils augment what people brought with them.

People eat standing on damp stones exposed by the tide, tossing shells back into the ocean. Corn husks mix with seaweed. People cluster on boulders. Some eat on the grass, some on the beach. Dogs of all color and shape join the feast.

I eat a potato from my bare hands, dipping directly into hot butter.

My chin is covered in clam juice, lobster meat, and beard from mussels.

My orgy of food, two plates completed and a third started, I hear the musicians tune again. The drummers limber their wrists on the drums.

I bend to the seawater. I wash my hands. I wash my face. I toss the last of my shells into the fire pit and the paper plate to the bonfire that blazes on Old Isaac's lawn. It is still hard to think of this house and land all belonging to Tad.

Others are dancing before I get there. They dance with greater energy, greater youth, more grace. Some lie on the grass. Some find darker places to bed.

The moon rises.

When I see it over the trees to the east, I lick Tad on the neck below his ear. I let a small, warm exhale caress that soft little area above his lobe. The impromptu band plays a waltz.

The open guitar case overflows with tens, twenties, fifties.

We have hours to go.

Moonlight shines on blanket-covered couples once hidden.

April, I think, *will be bountiful.* So many may think Dionysus rules the evening, but I know it is Brighid. Call her what you will: Brigid, Aphrodite, Ostara.

Players play on. Some quit. Others join. Singers of the village sing. The pace slows. The fire quiets.

12. tunc *tempo: andante*

I had time to think of my response. I needed to express surprise, but I had to make him feel welcome. Paul had travelled from Illinois to surprise me. No matter my true reaction, I had to honor his effort. I had often judged him a wimp for letting me go. He hadn't asked me to stay. He hadn't fussed with me. He had not probed into the greater reasons for my departure.

He'd watched me pack. He'd helped me put things into the red Volvo. He'd listened while I put a cardboard box out for my mail. "Put my mail in here until I get an address," I'd instructed him.

I was leaving, and he was treating it as if I were going to summer camp or just another business trip in a career of travelling and hustling. I know I hadn't told him all of what went on with my job changes that winter. He knew I was hurt. I could see the reflections of my own injuries in sadness he displayed on his face. We went through the process of my leaving almost silently. Oh, we talked about dinner and weekend plans and what to watch on TV. We left the core issues untouched.

I had told him that I would be back in three months. And he'd graciously taken me for my word. He'd let me go with grace. There is a fine line between grace and wimpiness. My mind would rest on one definition of his actions, then the other. At one moment, I thought his actions kind and gentle, and in the next, ineffectual.

Our departing kiss had not been one of passion. There was no longing in it. There were no hints of sex, no overtures of unstated promises. We gave each other chaste kisses. These were the kisses of long-married people. In reflection, I wonder if I'd seen that dreaded strategy: hope. Was that his approach? To hope I'd come back? Give me a few weeks away and hope I'd come home?

Well, I guess hope wasn't his complete strategy because there he stood, looping a bight over a bollard.

I certainly didn't want to have the mate see us kiss. He would turn that goodness foul. And yet, there stood Paul, with figuratively open arms, awaiting a warm, wet kiss and a grand hug. This mate, Samuel Selby, the bully of our little coast, wasn't going to disrupt what kindness I could offer my husband. Little Sammy can leer and jeer and poke at me when we put to sea again. I can take it. Better to be the fodder for Sammy's bullshit than to explain the mate to Paul.

There is no explaining why a person of my skills, age, and accomplishments would live among these problems — why she would do it deliberately. Better to tell Paul a rosy story and give him a few nice days.

I stepped off the schooner when she came to rest. His eyes and his face read a tentative, "Are you glad to see me?" All I could do was fall into his chest and let him hug me. I turned my face up to him for a kiss.

"I need to see the passengers off." We broke the embrace, and I helped set the gangway. The path down to the dock was steep since tide was at slack before the ebb. I stood at the bottom of the gangway, giving a hand to those who took it.

"B-bye now. Thanks for coming." I held Paul's hand while the passengers with their bags paraded past us.

With the five of them gone and a little hug for my teenager, I asked Paul, "How long will you be here? How much time have we got?"

"A couple of days, I guess. I was home alone on Wednesday, which was the Fourth. I went to see the fireworks alone, and so Thursday, I bought a ticket to historic Boston." The Black Swan had spent the Fourth of July watching the distant fireworks of Stoneybridge. People had told stories of the Fourths of July from their youth. The evening ended with a light drizzle.

"I think we head out tomorrow." I left off the, "unless they cancel," which I included in all my thoughts about scheduling. "Maybe you can join us for a couple of days at sea."

He mulled over the offer. "I met Mrs. Bayley. She seems nice. She said that you stayed there in late June."

"Martha? Yeah, I did. The rest of the crew had to go do safety maneuvers like man-over-board and the like. I was off playing in the launch and got left behind."

"You seem pretty well known. I met Raif, the bartender, too."

"Isn't he a great cook?"

"I guess so."

We were going around the issues again. "Would you like a tour?"

I took him aboard and showed him the deck and the galley. I showed him the tiny cubby that is my bunk: some eighteen cubic feet of personal space, a bunk separated by a small blue curtain. I showed him my head but didn't show him that I had to pump my poop down narrow piping. I left that bit out. The tour didn't take that long. He wasn't very interested.

"We could take a walk? I can take you down to a place I call Flat Rock. It's over there on the other side of the harbor."

We were standing on the deck when I was pointing out the proposed destination.

The mate walked up, and the captain was behind him, wearing a black T-shirt. They had both come for introductions, clearly.

"Paul, this is our mate, Samuel Selby. Sam, this is my husband, Dr. Paul Lapp." They shook hands. "And our captain, James Cobb."

"Doctor."

"Captain."

I could see that I had summarily ended the conversations. "I am going to take Paul around town. I'll see you later." My voice was cheery, as if I always told them what I was doing, as if we actually ever talked. I took Paul by the hand and walked down the gangway.

I think Martha was sincerely glad to see me stay at her place with my husband. We showed up after dinner. She greeted me like a friend and made very polite noises about my husband.

By breakfast time, Paul had decided not to join me for a three-day sail. I credit him with the confidence not to lie about some excuse. He just told me that he was going to head home, maybe see an old friend in Boston for dinner before hopping a flight back. I could feel his disappointment.

Frankly, I don't think any of my lies worked. I tried to frame the month of June in a positive way. I weaved little stories from the truth, creating a tapestry of my successes. And in his normal, nice way, he didn't call bullshit on my efforts. By breakfast, I think he had an honest assessment of my situation. This was no summer camp, no adult romp in the woods. I was just as miserable here as I had been at work during the winter. Nothing much had changed in the months: two months, three months, six months, eight months.

He probably knew the day, maybe even the hour, I learned I was losing my position as a front-line vice president. And now, in July, stories of the shenanigans our companies were playing had hit the news. My company wasn't yet in the papers. That was only a matter of time. WorldCom, Enron, and tumbling stock markets were all getting headlines. The cozy relationships with government to relax the laws were now under scrutiny: the Telecom Act of 1996 and the 1996 deregulation of energy companies by the Federal Energy Regulatory Commission. From the big picture, I had nothing to be ashamed of. I had been put out of a game that the nation was now judging as criminal. They had deliberately replaced me with a crook, a cheating, deceitful, and evil crook. And yet, that didn't soften the blow to my ego. I wasn't the one the board of directors and the senior VPs wanted to keep around. That gnawed at me.

We took another walk after breakfast, but we were already feeling our way through a slow goodbye. I was ready for him to leave. He was ready to leave. I needed more time alone. And he didn't express interest in spending more time with me. I felt he was more eager to leave than I was to have him leave, a reversal of roles for us.

There were two things on his mind. By noon, when he left, I knew them both.

During our walk, he politely and calmly asked if I were coming home. He politely called my leave of absence a lie, a lie that we were both now ready to admit. He knew my answer. I knew my answer. My mail had been coming to a post box here for a month now. Some bills were left at his address, but many of my personal items, my daily-used credit cards and cell phone bills came directly to me.

With the new rippling of the markets and the impact it was having on the economy, we were both able to admit that few high-tech companies would need a VP this minute. A recession was starting, and I was in the stands, watching. Not many jobs would be opening.

Returning home would be returning to something that we would both have to call unemployment. I'd dress it up. I'd consult. I'd do a bit of writing and the like, but day-to-day, I'd be unemployed. During the next months, my friends and my neighbors would be unemployed as well. This was not an environment my ego would be able to tolerate. I'd rather be a waitress in the Oar and Spar here than at home fiddling on a laptop, trying to make believe I was busy and important.

He knew that just as well as I did. He needed to hear the words. He needed me to call out my decision and say it with some honesty. I didn't.

I didn't. I finished the walk with him next to me, saying, "Paul, let me finish this summer and see where that takes me. I am just not ready to make any big decisions right now."

"Maggie, God knows I love you, but you made this decision months ago." I looked a bit shocked. He did it; he finally called bullshit.

"I need the summer."

"Maggie, you sold just about every single telecom and high-tech stock you had in November, December, and January. You cashed out of just about everything you could." I had. I really had. Just about everything that sat in individual stocks, I'd sold. I'd kept a lot in indexed funds and large mutual funds. But everything that I personally managed, I sold. I sold them because I was pissed. I was pissed off at the whole industry. Just about everybody I knew in business, I was pissed off at. Furthermore, I recognized that whatever was next wouldn't include my ability to track from the inside as I had been doing. I knew I couldn't manage stocks from Italy or the South of France. I didn't know then where I was going, but the idea of a leave of absence started to percolate. Stocks were high, and I was going on a personal low swing. My attitude was sell and be liquid. *I can always buy again when I am solidly on my feet.*

Regardless, the action of selling in November and leaving Illinois in early May certainly gave indications that I was operating off of a master plan, some grand scheme toward new goals. Clearly, Paul saw that.

I didn't feel very connected to any goals, any grand scheme.

We grabbed a beer and a sandwich at Raif's. Black Swan was in full view from the booth. When we watched the mate climb down off the dock to board, Paul said, "Be careful."

His eyes were on the mate, as if he could know about the mate's activities and nature. I doubted he knew. How could he? Out of politeness, I said, "I'll be fine. It's not what I expected. But it is good for me, for now."

We talked on and then sat in silence for a moment. I still had shopping to do and a boat to prep; he had a drive down the coast. He wouldn't make Boston in daylight. He could make it, but it would be very late when he got in. We walked to the car, hand-in-hand. I felt sad. I think he felt sad too.

He unlocked the rented Taurus with a push-button on the key fob, and I opened the door for him. I kissed him when he sat down.

"Be careful," he said again.

"I will be. I'm learning. I am getting the hang of this. Anyway, another month or two and it's over."

"No, Maggie, that's not what I mean. That mate is evil, and your captain is a heroin addict."

"What do you mean? About the captain . . . "

"His eyes, his skin. I think he has hepatitis as well. There are old needle scars on this arm, but he isn't shooting up there anymore. His pupils are pin-points. You don't need to be here, you know. You really don't."

And with that, he closed the door to the rental car and started the engine.

I shopped for six. I cleaned the icebox and loaded the blocks of ice. I exchanged the bedding, leaving the dirty stuff at the cleaners. I cleaned the heads and prepared for yet another trip down the coast—more wooded islands, more birds, more seals, another whale. My enthusiasm had dimmed. After two couples boarded, we got word that two people had cancelled. I gave my tour with a masked lethargy. I smiled. I put practiced intonation into my voice. I made eye contact. I bade them a good night. I returned to my galley, bringing to a close yet another episode of the Maggie Show.

I lay on my bunk, staring at the notes and graffiti of the former cooks.

I don't really know what monks and nuns think about cloisters, but I was beginning to get a sense of it. Being locked away in a world of deliberate silence and deprivation cannot be spiritual. There was a reason they called their little beehives and rooms cells. A prison's a prison. An eighty-foot boat with a bastard for a mate, a drug-addicted captain, and mumbling idiots for crew was a prison. The serenity of my galley, the serenity of my mind was some sort of sick lie. I was not at peace, not living in peace, nor striving to find peace.

I was hiding.

I was playing an adult's version of hide-and-seek. The difference between this game and the child's version was that, in the child's version, someone is actually seeking. Someone, a friend, calls out a name and does the searching. There's a game to be found both in the hiding and the seeking. I lay there, in my cell of a bunk, realizing that no one was actually seeking me. Paul had just left without a helpful word. He simply stopped by for some bland sex and left in his mid-sized rental car with Hertz NeverLost.

He didn't ask me to come home. He didn't make any promises of making things better. He pointed out where I had gone wrong and left. He cut his trip short, too. He could have stayed. He could have put to sea with us. Room wasn't a problem, clearly; neither was food.

With maturity, people let you alone. With age, the seekers stop seeking. The game was called "Hide," "Hide and Be Not Sought." There was a loneliness to this that I admitted. Hide and find yourself in a concealed, hidden place. Hide and find yourself at sea. Maybe the game is Run-and-Hide. Honestly, the fun is being sought, being wanted. Being needed.

If the game was hide-and-seek, I lost. No one chased. No one sought. No one found me. If the game was called only Hide, I still lost, for I was barely hidden. Everyday, a bit more was exposed and revealed. I lost because no one cared. Paul said, "Be careful," as if that was helpful.

Sleep left promises of change and bright days unfulfilled. I woke in the same state I fell asleep in: searching, lost, lonely, and not wanting anyone near.

I touched my stove. "Good morning."

I turned the primary fuel valve three full revolutions: one, two, three.

I bent and opened the secondary fuel valve. This valve opens the path to the plastic float-valve carburetor. The fuel from the deck trickled into the bottom of the firebox. The brick first dampened, then flooded. With the lid off the firebox, I watched.

I decided there was enough fuel. I twisted a paper towel into a loose rope and lit it. I dropped this into the firebox. A slow, cool fire started to burn.

After minutes, I turned on the blower, feeding the tender fire oxygen.

Maybe the secret to cloisters didn't come from being within a cell but working and giving the work one's entire focus. The challenge was to open the mind, let the concerns of the world float away. Ritual can be freeing. I was telling myself this: ritual can be freeing.

13. nunc — *tempo: andante*

I have scant hours to turn myself and this schooner around. I awake at zero-eight, and during the ensuing eight hours, prepare for a full boat of paying passengers.

I discover my mind far, far clearer than I had expected after a night of partying, my tongue, less like cotton than I deserve. My hips hurt. My hips hurt in a way that they haven't hurt in half a lifetime. The repeated climbs up my companionway and the climbs up from the boat to the dock are therapeutic.

I look forward to the passengers' arrival. It will bring an end to my climbing and hauling ice, food, frozen milk, meat, and laundry. The tide floods during the day. By the time folks start arriving, there is only a small step up to the boat. David and Joe both have foul hangovers. I pity them. I feel responsible to some mild degree. They aren't much good and certainly not much good to me. So I leave them alone, although I would appreciate their help. Nothing like a couple of young men who are willing to take direct orders and help haul stuff.

Stuart has been proving himself to be a decent mate. I let him be because Kieran lets him be. Kieran gives Stuart the boat to turn around on his own. I know it to be a bit of a test. I suppose Stuart does too. To his credit, he doesn't rush. He knows the time he has, and he uses it slowly and well. Kieran could do it faster and help me.

I find some comfort after the noon hour. I lie on my bunk, closing my eyes.

Maybe it is time to buy a house. I'm not coming to a sense of finality but rather a sense of comfortable flux. I ask myself, *What is the problem with having one lifestyle in the summer and another in the winter? Isn't that very, very traditional?* Coastal people move to fishing grounds. Herding people go up mountains to summer pastures. People move from the cities in the summer to avoid diseases and the heat. With a little planning, I could be a part of this work and life during the summer, then during the winter, go find other stuff to do: teach, study, travel.

This would be a commitment to a continuation of the activities I have already been doing. I certainly didn't show up on this coast as a licensed captain nor an EMT. I have become both since arriving here. With an odd smile, I think about lecturing at the business school at U. Maine in Orono. It is one thing to stand in a classroom and speak from an academic perspective, rambling on about business, ethics, finance, bottom lines, and the like. It would be rather a different perspective to have a somewhat battered campaigner, a veteran, stand at the front of a room. If I include summer jobs, internships, and this recent work here on the Black Swan, my career in business extends twenty-five to twenty-seven years.

I thought I would be napping. Instead I find myself sincerely exploring this idea. Maybe I'll buy a house down here and keep a small condo in Bangor or Orono, someplace within striking distance.

I could lecture on the perils and duties of leadership. During my time as a vice president, I wanted to try this little experiment. This was to be an experiment in the ridiculous. I wanted to ask a young manager, "When will the grass be green?" I really did. I figured if I asked in February, I'd get an answer of something like mid-March.

"I think we could get there in thirty to sixty days," he'd answer with confidence in his voice, a great belief in his own ability to accomplish any tasks given him.

"Really, how?"

"Well, forecasts are showing that the snow is letting up. If we get a few sunny days in early March and the snow abated, I am certain, with a little aggressive tending, we could get that old grass in shape pretty quick."

That is the hypothetical scenario based on a February start. With the same question, same test performed in late March, I'd ask, "When will the grass be green?" I'd ask this in the same manner, same flat intonation.

My hypothetical subordinate would likely say, "I think we can get there in a week, maybe two on the outside." No doubt, he'd get anxious in a few days, maybe even ask for weekend volunteers to have people snow-blowing snow from the lawns to the warmer asphalt.

These managers are so quick to assume. I found them so quick to leap without asking what it was I wanted. I don't know if I can explain this well. But for me to ask a benign question, lamenting the retarded pace of spring, is not a call to action. Some part of our training in business is to listen for the unmet, unstated need. Find the opportunity to do the impossible, to exceed your boss's expectation. That is the way to promotion and opportunity. Carry an attitude that declares, "There are no obstacles."

That is the American way in business. As Admiral Farragut said, "Damn the torpedoes." The irony of my experimental or hypothetical situation here is derived from two things. One is human nature. The other is the weather. No amount of supercharging, planning, tools, and money would be able to change the seasons. Yet we are taught to believe we can augment the gods. Hey, it's February in Illinois, and I think I can get green grass by mid-March. Rewards come from solving the impossible problems. To fail to plan contingencies in a business plan or a project plan for weather, shipping problems, part problems, resource problems, legal problems, is to fail in management. Therefore, if you can see a potential problem, then it is imperative to use necessary resources, tools, tricks, and efforts to work around that obstacle.

So here is my hypothetical manager, hard-charging, eager, capable, and wanting to shine. And there I sit in my office chair, looking at another gray winter's day. I might be thinking of Hawaii or the Greek Isles. I make an off-handed remark to a subordinate, and without further discussion, great efforts ensue. My young manager leaves my office and goes to his team saying, "Let's see if we can't get the grass green outside the boss's office by mid-March. I think it's do-able."

The green grass issue may seem a little over the top, but I can assure you that it isn't. My casual comments became imperatives for a team of people. I certainly didn't mean for them to become massive actions so that one young fellow could make himself look good, look the hero to me.

Once, I walked into a break room that looked a little tired: there were skid marks on the linoleum tiles where vending machines had been moved; the Formica counters had a few stains; the yellow walls looked just a little dirty, a little faded. This break room wasn't in my building. I was just passing by. I had a few managers in tow. I think we were looking for some office space for a new group that was joining our division. I simply looked around the room and said, "This room looks a little tired, doesn't it?"

I got digital photos and a task summary two weeks later. Contracts were let to the cleaning company. Paint was slapped up on the walls. New bulletin boards were purchased and mounted. The room looked clean and bright and so like all the rest of our corporate break rooms that I had two reactions. The first reaction was confusion. I had no idea why I was getting this report and these photos. I didn't care one bit. I had almost no recollection of making these statements, no real memory of seeing the room, the events surrounding the trip to this room, nor my comments when I did see it. I don't think I even stepped fully into this little break room. My second reaction was regret. What resources, time, budget, and lives did my comment disrupt? I wanted to know who lost weekends with family. What manager had to tell some employee, "Sorry, bud, no money. No raise. I'll fight for you next time around." All this because we spent money on a break room I saw in passing.

I didn't have the freedom to say, "Gee, I think green grass and spring would be nice about now. I am tired of snow." If you are the boss of bosses of bosses, such a trite statement becomes the battle cry of a horde. I wasn't free to make a comment about the condition of a break room without people undertaking to change it immediately.

You'd think someone would say, "Ma'am, green grass is nice. That snow is getting really crusty and old. I, too, am dying for some color." I'd come back and say, "It's Illinois. It'll be over when it's over, I guess." And we'd return to our work.

But no, people charge off and guess at what is needed. And they try to make the world move just that much faster. "Green grass next week, ma'am. Tough to do in January, but you've got the right team here."

"She was aghast at the condition of this break room. We need to make changes right away. Fire the current cleaning crew. Get a new one in here. Get facilities to paint the walls." I can only imagine the real conversation and the real impact on people.

As a result, I learned to keep my damn mouth shut. These people couldn't imagine my reaction if they had a real conversation with me. So rarely did anyone ask the next question, "Would you like something done about this?" Most of the time, my answer would have been no.

Who knows if I was a force for good or not? No great books will be written about my tenure as a vice president, at least no books written by others.

If given the chance to stand in a room with bright, shiny students, there would be at least two lessons: one, hope is not a strategy; two, ask the next question. There would be another lesson about getting tasks in the right order. Most of us do learn this early on: rape, pillage, then burn. Order does matter. Consequences instruct on that lesson well.

I think I ought to stand in a room and teach this stuff.

"Hey, Cookie?" My eyes had been closed while I pondered.

"What?" Kieran calls for me from the companionway hatch. That normally means I am needed up top. I drop from my bunk and into my leather Teva sandals.

"Meet the Family Johnson: Adam, Mary. Their taller stud is George and the towhead is . . . No, I'll get it—Ned. Ahh, the towhead is Ned, I've got it now. All, this is our cook and your guide through the next week or so, Margaret Noonan."

"Hello, hello, hello, hello." I offer each a handshake and a personal hello. "Welcome aboard. We'll get you situated. Take your kit and follow me."

I meet people. I give tours. I point them toward dinner. By eight, I am sound asleep in my little bunk. I don't even hear Tad and Raven enter the galley. At 4:30, I find a note on my stove:

Got an e-mail from Lyttle Shipyard. August 15th still looks good for them. You were so peaceful, I didn't have the heart to disturb you. Hope you slept well. You did a good thing yesterday. We'll talk about Maggie's Clambake for years to come. Thank you for that . . .

14. tunc

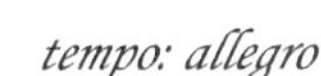

I woke in the grips of an unceasing curiosity. Paul's visit left me with a sense of disconnect to this crazy boat I was calling home. Certainly, there were things about her I didn't understand, but there was something I was coming to understand: she had a history.

This old schooner had two personas: an honest one and a not-so-honest one. One was certainly called Black Swan. Then there were these little tricks: hull numbers that reversed, hidden cashes, removable nameboards. Although I hadn't explored the transom, I had to guess that the large nameboard there also could be removed with a quick movement. This would be like changing flags while sailing in enemy territory or donning a disguise.

I woke with a sense of wonder. *Who is the Black Swan masking? What is her alter-ego's name?* With these questions firmly established, waking brought clarity. *If I were to hide signboards for the other persona,* I asked myself, *where would I hide them?* The answer was obvious, well, not that obvious. If I hid them, I would put them in the companionway. Easy access, well hidden, revealed only when changing the name.

With seven passengers on board, I got the stove lit — boom, boom, boom — no fuss, fuel on, twisted towel, small, cool fire. I then climbed halfway up the companionway steps and opened the sliding hatch to a light, drizzling rain. I turned around to face the hull number. I removed it easily and felt the cavity. I explored the sides of the cavity with a great sense of expecting to find alternate nameboards for her bows. Sure enough, they were held snuggly in place. They were upright in small tracks. I pulled one out. It read: RAVEN.

Black Swan, Raven, Black Swan. Hull number: 6010861 and hull number: 1980109. Rain dripped down the back of my shirt, down my spine, and into my pants. I slid the companionway hatch cover closed after I put the signs away.

I so wished for an Internet connection. I was two days from tying up at the dock. I would have spent time on Google. Then I would have drafted a few e-mails off to folks. Does Lyttle Shipworks still exist? Do they have records of building the Black Swan? Clearly, the owners of the Black Swan and her ship builders were in cahoots with each other. This boat had to have been built deliberately for her intended purpose: smuggling. These niches and well-designed name changes would not have been done as elegantly after construction. Actually, my previous explorations showed that during her refit to hauling passengers, many niches were removed. I started looking forward to getting ashore again, getting to the little stone library and having a chat with Dale Abernathy. He may have been a cop and chief of police, but he was also a descendant of the current owner.

If I could have pushed the boat back to the harbor, I would have. I still had to go through the motions of the sea days ahead: making bread, preparing meals, cleaning, serving, and entertaining folks. My galley would be full during a lousy, rainy day such as this. On a day such as this, people would play Monopoly. Then they would fight over vocabulary while playing Scrabble. They'd get a bit bored and a little stir-crazy.

Sailing down east toward our harbor and our dock brought me some relief. I had another quick turnaround. My focus ought to have been on food, laundry, cleaning and preparing —ought to have been, and was. But even with tasks, there are always a few minutes to poke around.

I took the bed linen to the laundry and headed to the library. Google revealed nothing useful, not even a website for the company. I climbed down the infernal links in Yahoo! to find Sturgis Cove, Maine. I found listings for the family name, Lyttle. I found businesses such as hardware stores and hairdressers. I found nothing about a boatyard in that area. There were no listings for Lyttle Shipyard in the online phone books. I searched both the region and Sturgis Cove.

I had to admit, after my months spent down east, the absence of a banner on the old information highway doesn't prove much. One can exist, live, and thrive (in a way) here on this coast without a website advertising yourself to the greater World Wide Web. One can own a boatyard here without having a phone listing, without advertising, and without a Web site.

I decided to catch Dale before the business day ended. I walked from the library to the town hall. Once in, I headed down to the far end of the hall. Under the small sign that read: *Police*, I stopped.

"Good afternoon, I'm looking for Dale Abernathy." The officer at the desk happened to be the officer that responded to the fight between the mate and David.

"What do you need him for?" Clearly, he remembered me too.

"I don't need him for anything, based on the strict definitions of need. But I would like to speak with him." I can recognize my own surly nature.

"He's not down here right now. Leave your name, and he'll call you."

"Tell you what. I'll leave my name. It's Margaret Noonan, as you may remember. And as for my phone number, he doesn't need it. He can just look out the window. If the Black Swan is here, I am in town. If she isn't, I am gone. There is no phone." I was being a bitch now. I didn't often get to do this much anymore. I sort of enjoyed it.

I pulled a business card from my pocket: "May I use your phone? I'll call him. I have his home phone, his cell, and his office number."

"He's upstairs."

I leaned back out the window, and kitty-corner from me, with a clear placard sticking into the hallway like all the other doors, hung a 1930s style sign: *Stairs*.

I left without saying thank you.

I knocked at Dale's door. Then I let myself in without waiting for an answer: what would a small town cop have going on? I sat in his guest chair. "Tell me about Raven."

He gave me a peculiar look. I continued, "Raven is the alter ego of your great uncle's boat. Within five minutes the crews of old could have changed her name from Black Swan to Raven. I am just wondering what the story is behind it."

He smiled broadly, almost giving me a bit of a laugh. "I thought I sent you on a mission to discover the present problems."

"Okay, okay, I still haven't committed to that. I never said yes, did I? This is more interesting anyway, isn't it?"

"No. That's just history."

"Interesting history."

"Stories. That's all."

"Stories, like what?"

"Stories like what I still hear." I believed he was referring to the current smuggling he suspected the crew engaged in.

"Past and present are connected."

"Yes, but no. Someone else is using that boat for his own gains. The world is different now. People just don't wink and nod at a bit of hidden cargo. A little contraband helped keep this coast vibrant. I acknowledge that, not exactly a proud tradition. Not exactly legal, but that was then."

"Okay, I'll snoop a little for you. Not too much. They're not nice guys." I opted not to share my doctor-husband's diagnosis of the heroin problem. That sort of news would have brought the summer to an immediate end. I wasn't ready for the beach yet.

"Don't you have a boat to turn around?" His words meant, "go away, now." But like so much of what he said, the words didn't match the kindness and humor he showed me with his face and his actions. Talking with him made me feel just a little out of balance. Words and attitude didn't match. Dale affected this casual, loose approach while trying to conceal a steely nature; he affected an attitude of not knowing information when he seemed to actually have the inside poop.

"Yes. I'm pretty practiced. It doesn't take me that long."

"Herm." He nodded. His messages were mixed. He talked and acted sternly, yet there seemed to be a childishness about him.

I took a risk and played back. "Don't get so snippy with me, Don Abernathy, under-boss of the Abernathy crime family. You just use this cop-thing as a cover. I'm starting to see who you really are."

I turned to walk out, and he spoke to my back.

"Raven isn't an alter ego but an identical sister boat. They were twins." He paused, then added, "Be careful out there."

I closed his door.

Three-card monte played with two large black schooners must have keep the revenuers busy for decades. There is a certain criminal freedom left to twins. Even today with the use of DNA, courts and juries have a difficult time making legal distinctions between twins.

Required legal certainty disappears when possibilities appear. Was it Tim or Tom who raped Betty? Betty, the victim, can't tell the difference, and neither can the scientists with the DNA. Tim (or Tom) was clearly seen by many at the bank during the hours Betty was molested. One is innocent. One is guilty.

Was it the Black Swan or not that entered the harbor? Or Raven? All the rest of the distinguishing factors can be modified. Crews and officers can change boats mid-course; cargoes can be transferred. In the days before radar, aerial surveillance, satellite imagery, audio surveillance with hydrophones, and the other skookum applications of technology, activities at sea were invisible to officials. Once a vessel sailed out of sight, it was behind an imaginary curtain. She disappeared from all eyes ashore.

I thought of the Gary Larson cartoon in which cows are standing on two legs, talking in a field. Then, one of them spots a car and its cargo of humans. In the next frame, the cows are on four legs, mooing and docilely eating grass. What goes on beyond our horizons are big unknowns. Mermaids could be sunbathing. Whales may be frolicking on the surface. Giant monsters may exist, perpetually out of sight. To the landsmen, the mile past the horizon conceals mystery.

Events should logically flow from one to another. It is in the infant mind that events are noncontiguous. With childhood games of peek-a-boo, we learn that what goes away should / will likely / may often come back. As we grow, we learn that things do go missing. Things do go away. But we have to explain that as an anomaly. We have to learn what an absence is. We have to have absence explained to us. Our rule book says things don't just disappear. There is also a rule that things don't just appear. That violates our sense of natural order, our sense of physics.

We draw mental straight lines between things. We accept the simplest explanation that fits the data. We celebrate Occam's razor. We celebrate rules of parsimony. If we've never seen the cows in the field stand and talk and we've seen a lot of cows over a lot of years, then it is unlikely that, because I turn my back, cows are standing and talking. It just doesn't fit our understanding of the world.

But that is the trick behind three-card monte. We see the ace of spades. We see exactly three cards, yet we never pick the ace of spades. The more intelligent know that this game is not about finding the ace of spades. It is a sleight of hand, often, a sleight of hand that is hiding yet another sleight of hand. With three-card monte, no matter how well you watch, no matter how well you play, you cannot win. If you do find the ace, you'll shortly find that your wallet has been picked. Win a few bucks, and you'll be mugged at the next corner. For you just showed all where you kept your money. We focus on the movement, the cards, and the flash.

What we don't see is the intent. Someone wants your money, your wallet, and to get that, they will take your attention. They hide their ambition. They entertain with a talent from the street. With the regular pitter-patter practices of street dazzle, with the skill of a carnival barker, the shuffle of three cards on a cardboard box, everything in front of you is saying, "Look here!" "Watch," "Look! See this?" Your mind follows the game, trying to make a parsimonious deduction as to the location of the ace. That is the point, isn't it?

The players know we are trying to make sense of an imperfect world. They make understanding harder for their mark (you). The mark is trying to pull together facts and observations that don't necessarily make sense. And in that moment of suspended illusion, the players have tremendous freedom. They are behind a figurative curtain of their own making.

Get taken in a game of three-card monte, and you feel victimized twice. You've lost money, and you take the blame on yourself. "I should have known better." This is far more entertaining than meeting some thug on the street who threatens and steals. There is a cleverness we admire, a bit.

The corporate world plays some of the same games. People have funny books, business deals that cross-revenue and never yield a product, lease-in/lease-out, pyramid schemes. All of these share characteristics with the basic street hustle. They involve distraction and a sleight of hand. They involve people seeing what they want to see. People put together the facts in such a way that it makes sense; they see the good in others.

If I don't believe that cows stand up and talk when I am not looking, then they don't. Even if they do, even if I saw it, I'd have to be convinced to believe it. I'd have to reconcile this observation with thousands of years of collective study, understanding, and physics. Cows just don't stand up.

They don't have the hips for it.

If I saw a cow stand up and talk, I just wouldn't believe it. I would dismiss the data. I would think something was wrong with me, with my observations, with my mind. I would doubt myself, not the world. The rules of our physics and our understanding always apply first.

Thus, we build little domains of faith. We believe that no great mystery exists beyond our personal horizons. The physics one mile beyond what I can see follow the same rules as the physics I know right here and right now. So, if one chooses to change the rules, this is the place to do it. Do it just out of sight, but nearby. Do it with a bit of distraction. Conceal with a sleight of hand. Create a figurative curtain that hides what needs to be hidden, and reveal only that which you want revealed. Play with the faith of those who watch. We won't believe it. We will interpret what we are seeing by the rules we have spent a lifetime understanding: things don't just disappear and appear; things in the next minute will resemble this minute.

Like the players on a street corner or a carnival barker, this boy who took my VP job stood in meetings saying, "Oh look, here's fifty million dollars worth of revenue." They all watched him with his shuffle and jive. But for all his noise and effort, we might have just printed our own money. We borrowed fifty million, okay. That is what it should have been called. That fifty million was not revenue but liability — a liability dressed in revenue's clothing. A quick shuffle, a little distraction, a sleight of hand, the collaboration of the others on our street corner. All together we fleeced the unsuspecting visitor in our land. We fleeced our mark. We took money from investors, from banks, and from leasing companies. We used a three-card monte that concealed sham holding companies, bogus transactions, and our intent. They just want to make sure you are watching the game. Focus on the game! Are we playing by the rules? Do your rules still apply? Are we following the law? You didn't see that? We'll do it again! Meanwhile, they are picking pockets and taking what they want.

It's a trick, a trick of distraction, of sleight of hand, of speed, of officious banter. As long as you are looking where we want you to look, we are completely free. We are, in fact, invisible.

The Black Swan and the Raven were doing a bit of smuggling razzle-dazzle: a two-card monte, played on the New England coast. And if the official world never knew that two identical boats were built, then one would always be invisible.

But how could there be two boats with two registered names and one not be known to the officials?

That answer came easily: razzle-dazzle in two places. Have one boat behave as if it were from Canada and the other from the US. One boat would be Canadian, free to come and go from Canadian ports without inspections and official inquiry. The other would be from the US, free to come and go from US ports without inspections and official interaction. As a hypothesis, I started to believe this to be entirely true.

The Raven could tell all that she is sailing from Halifax, Nova Scotia to Yarmouth, to Grand Manan Island, then to St. John, New Brunswick. The Black Swan could tell all that she was starting a circuit from Portsmouth, New Hampshire sailing to Penobscot Bay then on down to Machias, Maine. Then, there in the middle of the Gulf of Maine, they could swap cargo, or swap boats, or swap crew.

No one could tell that the Black Swan ever left the US. No one would ever suspect the noble Raven departed from her path (by much). They could swap destinations. The Raven could sail from Yarmouth to Machias, reporting in as the Black Swan. The Black Swan could sail into St. John as the Raven. They'd never have to meet. They could transport goods, contraband, and cash going both directions. The ruse was elegant.

This was all a guess, of course.

I sat in my car, losing interest in the store. I pulled my cell phone from the glove box and dialed Dale's cell phone number.

"Dale, Margaret Noonan."

"Yes?"

"Did the Raven sail under a Canadian flag?" I posited my guess out loud.

"Yes." I could imagine a pleased look on his face.

"That's it." I hung up.

I went to the store to buy supplies for another trip.

"All right folks, since I have all of you together, I'll introduce myself. I am the cook, and essentially, your steward. My name is Margaret Noonan. Before we go below, we'll do a quick tour of this schooner.

"The Black Swan was built at the end of the nineteenth century in a shipyard not far from here. She seems to have been made for hauling cargo with modifications to optimize her ability to participate in illegal trading: running liquor and smuggling other contraband had been her purpose in life until she was converted to transport passengers for wind jamming

"She seems to carry with her a truly American spirit, a free will that I have come to admire. Smuggling has been a significant source of revenue for this area since the English colonized these shores centuries ago. Did you know that, in an effort to make the colonists dependant on English trade goods, the English forbid the local manufacture of iron goods such as shovels and ploughs? A locally made shovel was a wooden shovel. That was before the War for Independence, which ended in 1783. Jefferson's Embargo Act of 1807 essentially made criminals of all traders along these shores.

"The basic environment for smuggling includes: international borders, conflict, and imbalances across the border, all of which exist right here. From the French and Indian Wars, through our revolutionary period, the War of 1812, and the Neapolitan era, into our Civil War, then the Spanish American War, this coast has seen strife. Goods and services are needed. Laws are written to forbid their transport. Smuggling is the only resolution.

"Little did the owners of the Black Swan know that within a few years of her being put to sea at the turn of the previous century, the US Federal Government would be creating an entire new market for smuggling with Prohibition.

"We may look back on these old days with some romanticism. Who would think that prohibiting the import of metal shovels and huge taxes on tea would be a factor in creating a new government, a new nation? We now know that it is not immoral (or illegal) to have a drink at the end of a day or serve liquor at a party. But it was illegal for a number of years. Smuggling coasters such as Black Swan brought us that illegal liquor. You might think with NAFTA, who really needs smuggling, right? Smuggling is the domain of the truly bad such as drugs and human cargo."

I had re-drafted my introductory speech. I scanned my small audience to gauge their interest and participation.

"Well, we are all reading about folks running to Canada to buy medications. And those of us who live near the border know that Canadian toilets have higher volume and actually flush in one effort. Their shower heads have some umph to them. Our government has enacted a bunch of laws that limit water flow through toilets and shower heads. So, now, some US citizens run to Canada to buy thirteen-liter-per-flush toilets instead of the one-point-six-gallon-per-flush we are mandated to buy here. I'd argue smuggling is still alive and well along the gloriously open and free border between the US and Canada.

"This fore-hatch takes you to the fo'c'sle. This is the crew's private place. Please only go there if you are invited. As you sail, we'll introduce you to the lines and their functions: jib halyard, flying jib halyard, sheets, and the rest. This middle hatch is the opening to the galley . . . "

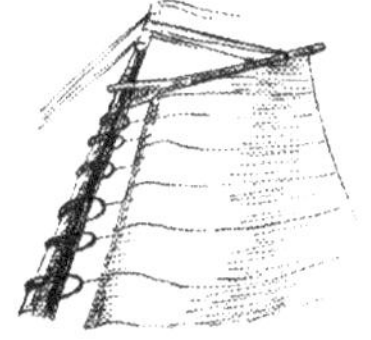

15. nunc — *tempo: adagio*

I have been living and working in a world without significant electrical power, without significant engines. Week after week, I use my car to haul food from the store to the boat. When I'm done with the car, I park it at Tad's house, and then I walk back to the boat.

I walk. I find great joy in walking. I see the opening of the roses. I watch the bloom develop on the roadside berry plants. I see the Queen Anne's lace and the daisies. I smell the chamomile. My feet feel the road, the dirt, and the rocks. I measure distance by telephone poles behind me or telephone poles in front of me.

I learn when local farms slaughter. With my occasional purchases of these local meats, I feel a greater connection to the rhythms that surrounded me. Even just the small process of planning my shopping trips around the tides allows me to feel connected to the greater world. I have learned to avoid shopping when the tides are low. With a neap tide low, I have to swing down a shroud before hitting the railing, a drop of a couple of feet. With a spring tide low, I have to climb down rigging to put my feet on the rails. I time my shopping days such that I step from the dock to the boat with a full load of groceries when the rail and the dock are roughly at the same level. It only takes planning and some attention to the lunar clock.

It takes understanding spring tides and neap tides and lunar cycles. Failure results in more work. Dropping groceries and ice down ten feet requires the use of a halyard rigged with a cargo net. We lay grocery bags into the net and gather the corners. These are attached to the bitter of the halyard, hoisted off the dock, and lowered to the deck. This is a very nineteenth century technique. And here we are, loading plastic grocery bags and frozen milk, very twenty-first century commodities.

My feet have grown rough over the years, not just tough enough to walk on barnacled rocks, but rough. They are callused, tanned, and have a texture like sandpaper. I think about the process of dressing in business clothing again, of having to put on girl shoes again. The idea makes me shudder. My feet would shred delicate shoes, not to mention the impact they would have on nylons.

"It should be a great sail," I announce to the morning group in the galley. We are about to put out to sea. "I've got seasick patches for folks. I encourage people to try them for the first day or so. There'll be a briefing by the captain, then by me. We'll untie and pull into the harbor. You guys ready?"

I can measure the eagerness and joy on nine bright faces.

"Go on, I'll be up in a second." I stack the dishes in a white plastic tub in my sink. I let it fill about one quarter of the way up with water. I drizzle some soap. I wash the galley table. I then head to the deck with a partially stowed galley.

Kieran is well into his practiced speech. I give my banter about rules and sponges. Lines are hauled and the diesel engine kicks into gear. We leave behind the mosquitoes and the noise of town. We leave behind cell phone towers (and therefore cell phone reception). We leave the Internet and TVs behind. Kieran takes a gentle left after passing nun number five. After three years, this process is like pulling out of the driveway. Our planning involves our destination: left or right. We scour the Internet and newspapers for little festivals. We track the migration of whales. We call others in the coastal tourist trade, looking for rooks that are bursting with birds, active seal haul-outs, and pods of sundry cetaceans.

I have the dishes finished when Kieran heads into the wind. I head to the deck.

"Come on, I'll take the ladies. We'll race."

Kieran picks up on my idea. "Men, back here with me. Joe!"

"David!" I holler. "David and I are going to show you our technique for hauling lines. Doing this well, you can get three people per line. That's a great deal of strength. David and I will face each other. Our arms alternate and are well above our heads." David and I make full, slow pulls. "Grab high, pull low, but stand up. The first bit is speed. Your third team member is on the tail. She takes a wrap like this on the belaying pin." I address Loretta. "Your job is to keep taking the slack out."

Of course, this won't go well.

"We need two teams of three. I'll take you two with me on the throat halyard. You three, on the peak halyard." David frees the fore sheet. He'll provide coaching and help tail the peak halyard.

Kieran has his team set up on the heavier main halyards. One halyard goes to the throat of the gaff, the other to the peak of the gaff. He has two on the peak halyard and three on the throat halyard. Joe is at the helm. I holler out, "Ready?"

"Ready, Cookie."

In a raspy whisper, I yell, "Go!" The women tangle arms. pulling with great enthusiasm. The throat gets well ahead of the peak. David stops my group to help the peak team get situated again. I watch the peak rise comfortably above the throat. "All right ladies, put your ovaries into it. Let's go." The sails make gentle, thunderous sounds. Joe keeps our nose into the wind and thus the pressure off the sails while we hoist.

“Time to horse, ladies. David, let’s show ’em.” We situate the folks who are tailing. We make one partial figure eight on the pin. “Hold that tight.” David and I start to horse in the line. I take the line in both hands and fall backward, using both my weight and my legs to make a horizontal pull. It’s like I’m knocking an arrow in a bow.

“As I relax, take up the slack,” I bark at Loretta, a passenger. One, two, three times, we horse the line in. I push backwards with my legs and weight. Loretta takes up the slack while I relax the line to its normal state. Each time, Loretta improves her timing and her ability. I take the line from her, make a couple of figure eights on the pin, and then make a locking loop.

“See that.” I undo and redo. The women are all watching me. David is dressing the peak halyard on this own. “Loretta, wanna try that?”

Her figure eights are a bit loose. She struggles, getting the last, locking loop the right way. “Good.” Then we coil. “Line has a lay. This is not like your garden hose, and it is unlike the braided line of modern yachts. It coils well one way. And it acts like a snake the other.

“There is none of this wrapping around the elbow and hand like it’s an extension cord. That only kinks a line. On this boat, we coil line clockwise on the deck. Make nice large, relaxed loops. You can almost toss the line. See. Smaller lines, these you might be able to do over your forearm. But the halyards are so much easier to coil on the deck.” I bend, pick up the coil, and with a flick of my wrist, I pull a bight from behind. I press the coil against the belaying pin and lock it in place. The movement was too quick for most to see. “That takes a little practice. As we sail, we’ll get you all jazzed up on the language and the skills.”

“Are we sailing?” asks Loretta.

“Yes, we are.”

“But we’re going faster now than we were with the engine.”

"And that is just the way it is on the beautiful Black Swan. She loves the wind."

People scatter to the corners of our small, steel world. I start bread, returning to the deck between each episode: mixing, kneading, and rising. I also start to prepare a rib roast of beef. I have recently been buying coarse-ground spice rubs from a spice house in Chicago. These have a wonderful old-world richness to them. I loved the feel of them between my hands on the meat.

A gentle, long swell rolls in from the west of us, while we sail northeast on a brisk breeze from the east. The movement, given the Black Swan's long, graceful hull, is pleasant. A smaller boat would have been tossed about. We slice. We cleave the water. I can hear excited little barks of joy from the passengers when the spray travels the full length of the deck.

There is no point of perpetual stasis. While sailing, there is an effort to balance the forces that drive. One can sail "in the slot" for a moment or an hour, but change will happen: wind, current, tides, land, something. Sailing in this narrow groove of trim, wind, and water, things are grand.

I am feeling as if I am "in the slot" for this moment. I am suspended, for the moment, within a balance of the forces around me. My mother isn't haunting. Paul isn't judging. Questions about my future are quiet. I am simply at sea, cooking a meal for a crew of happy people.

Tad and I have just over thirty days before we unveil the next step in our crazy little plan.

I like risks. Risks are fun.

A FedEx package is in Ralph's hand when we enter BATS at the end of the trip.

Ralph calls out to me, "Maggie, dear, I think this may be the package you have been . . . expecting?"

Expecting, yes. Wanting? Not really. Maybe. Still confused, I guess. You don't get divorced by accident, do you?

I left Paul. I packed my kit, took six-month's leave of absence from my job in Illinois, drove down the driveway, found I-90 east, and landed here.

Tad's grandfather, Isaac Abernathy, had been the owner of the Black Swan. It was Isaac who hired me. Isaac provided me an address to forward mail. I provided Paul, my husband, with a box into which mail could go. I'd spent twenty-something years in big business, twenty-something years living in proper houses, most of them with Paul, twenty-something years buying cars when I wanted to, twenty-something years working around rules, creating opportunities, and wiggling my way into jobs, twenty-something years of knowing what I was doing, where I was going, and who I was, and forty-something years believing that divorce was a sin, a failure on my part, and a failure to serve god.

Paul knew my departure was permanent long before I did. There was a look when I left, a look of resignation. He accepted my departure. He accepted the departure for what it was. He knew then I would not be back. He knew that I had lied to myself. And yet, there stood Paul, waving gently. Paul had the wisdom, maturity, and intelligence to let me tell myself these lies: sabbatical, a fall-homecoming, a renewal of interests, and a restoration of faith.

I love him even more for letting me go. He understood that clinging would have been an end without hope. Letting me drift allowed for hope.

I struggle to define humanity. At times, I see us as if we are water. We are fluid; we drift and flow. Who we are is ever changed by where we are. Our relationships give us form. We flow to fill gaps. As water, who we are is defined by where we came from; elements from each of our tributaries suspend within us. We have infinite capacity, infinite shapes, and infinite beauty.

When I envision us as water, I see us as clear water, formed like humans, formed yet fluid, clear yet not transparent. I see us as seawater, formed with legs, a head, arms that move, eyes that blink, and a mouth that breathes, a water-person, pinched from a semisolid form of liquid water.

Unlike fabric, we do not unravel with the tug of a thread. Unlike fabric, you cannot follow our elements to our source. With water, you cannot see the source of each droplet, of each mineral, of each molecule. Each is alone but bound to its neighbors. Far more complex than any tapestry, our structure is transparent, our bonds, invisible. Little gems, little impurities, little irritations carried within exist without being seen. We absorb our experiences. We absorb bits of what we touch without being linked to their source. Water does this. This is a property of water.

Experiences make up the great part of our whole being. As a water-person, I carry parts of my mother, my father, my grandmother, my cousins, and my teachers, all within. No one can simplify my being by studying who I am and drawing straight lines to these people and times. Connecting the dots in a life would create a confusing scribble-person, a mass of lines without form, without flexibility, without the very fluidity that allows us to change.

Yet, there stood Paul in our driveway, seeing me depart as if I were a scribble-person, as if lines connected my future and my past, as if he could see both the sources and the destinations. Driving east on I-90, I pulled and pulled and pulled and pulled a line that connected us. With time and distance separating us, the strength of this line became weaker. Here, three years and two months later, came the document that broke a connection that can never be broken. Part of me will always be in Illinois. We are not fabric.

I guess that's the difference between a scribble-person and a water-person. A water-person cannot be in two places. A scribble-person can exist all over the place, with messy boundaries and lines connected helter-skelter. On the other hand, a water-person appears self-contained. Paul, my mother, and Illinois exist always within me, absorbed, suspended, and awash within a space we call a soul, a memory, a heart.

This FedEx document changes me, and it doesn't change me. It changes me because it becomes a part of who I am. I am divorcing. And yet divorcing doesn't change who I am. I can't go in and remove the bits of Paul suspended within me, the bits of Paul that will slosh around, appearing and disappearing for the remainder of my life. And like the mysteries of quantum mechanics, these Paul-bits will remain connected and in sync with Paul even when separated. In quantum mechanics, there are these little quanta-bits that spin and remain synchronized well past boundaries of time, space, and understanding.

It is no different for us.

A FedEx package with divorce papers doesn't instantly change my relationship with Paul or the little Paul-flecks I carry. These papers give honesty to the truth we've discovered. We had gradually become unmarried. Slowly becoming unmarried is not so different from the graduated steps we take when we become married.

Once upon a time, we met. We'd see each other in the presence of friends. Then we dated. From meeting to marriage, our love waxed over three years. We supported and cherished each other.

Our marriage started its wane the day my mother died. I can see that connection now. My relationship with Paul had grown quiet and stale long before my mother died. Still, the marriage remained strong, strong until she died.

"Well, lass. Is it the divorce?" Kieran poses the question gently.

I still hold the thin pouch in my hands, unopened.

"I guess. I don't really know."

As they discuss Black Swan, I quietly open my FedEx pouch.

David watches.

Kieran, Stuart, and Tad all make a point of not watching. They discuss the engine and the computerized navigation systems they are upgrading.

"Raif, how about a little something for each of us." There is no need to give the man specifics; we each have our favorites.

"Let's toast Margaret's new freedom."

Is it a new freedom? I am not willing to redefine the meaning of signing the divorce papers. I am dreading that divorce may be less free than my marriage ever was. Paul gave me great freedom in our lives together. Although I never actually strayed from the marital bounds, I did stretch them over the years. The freedom I enjoyed was both in the resilience of the boundaries and the rigidity of the rules to which we must comply.

I sought the comforts and security of the marriage as much as I explored their very limits. I am not just talking about sexual encounters. Some men would have regarded my travel, my ambitions for promotion, and some of my pursuits a distraction from a marriage. Marriage also gave me mobility within the corporate culture I might not have had if I were single. Paul's status and his education benefited my career. I had tremendous freedom in our marriage.

Certainly, deciding to come east wasn't part of some greater argument with Paul. He opened his arms and let me go. He always had. That was freedom, freedom to come home, snuggle, whine, share, watch TV, freedom to armor myself with a dry-cleaned business suit and stiff shoes and march into a conference room. I took the best of both worlds: the freedom to make dinner and not make dinner. This was no white Hanes T-shirt clad husband who expected dinner at 6:20 each evening. Paul embodied kindness, gentility, and humility.

It is loneliness that traps us. It is loneliness that exposes our greatest fears. It is loneliness that can imprison us far more securely than love. Loneliness robs our strength, our skills, and our courage. With love, we see the world as our particular friend. While in the arms of love, we see opportunities abound.

The emotional leap that I don't understand came with the death of my mother. The judgment of culture, family, and tradition never released before explored thoughts within me—a freedom I am only now beginning to understand.

"To a free woman!"

The men stand. Tad, with his old-fashioned manner and old-fashioned style, says, "To a free woman!"

After a sip, I speak. I work a smile through my dense thoughts. "Let's clarify. A woman may be available. She shall never come free." Tad blushes. But Kieran, who does notice, leaves the issue untouched. "I'd like to propose a toast to my husband, my ex-husband, and my friend, Paul."

"To Paul." Tad offers a far more subdued tone.

The pouch contains exactly what it ought to contain: multiple copies, each with signature and date blocks. Paul has signed and dated these documents a week ago. The witness block for his signature is also complete. Conversation has stopped, replaced by a somber silence, a silence defined by the glistening in my eyes. Both Tad and Kieran lay a hand on my shoulder. I blink, and one tear eases onto my left cheek. Oh well, water-people are allowed to leak some, I guess.

Little memories of Paul and our years together are not the thoughts that opt to percolate. I come, instead, to remember the first glimpse of the Black Swan. I recognize the hope I then held for a better future. Changes don't come in an instant. We may find little meters of change: a storm, a full moon, a document, a license, a holiday, a death, and a birth. These are not events unto themselves, but they represent a spectrum of time. I force my mind back to Paul and away from memories of my mother's words.

The tear creeps down my cheek before I wipe it with my hand. Tad touches my neck with a gentle stroke. Kieran gives a little squeeze.

And so with a pen, I sign the documents. Paul will always be here, the signature on these documents and the witnessing by Kieran. With the signature, I release her. I release my mother. I let her go. I am not saying that a turn of phrase or an odor from the galley won't bring a memory and a tear back like a rogue wave. With this signature, I thee depart.

Raven takes to my heels when I leave the bar. I had signed the papers wordlessly and kissed both men next to me, each on his cheek, each as a substitution for the words "thank you." Those words would trigger a real cry. Better to leak a few tears and walk into the gloaming than sit here and cry out loud. How would I explain grieving my mother while severing my marriage to Paul?

Raven bounces happily while we walk east.

Darkness has come, and I still lie on Flat Rock. A rounded belly of the earth's skeleton forms to catch sun most of the day. Dry, warm, and smooth, Flat Rock provides a place to ponder the little questions, to nap, and to watch twilight rise from the east. The sun moves past our horizon, and he draws a line, or rather, casts a shadow, of earth's horizon, the horizon west of us. The last of the light is gone when the sun has sunk beyond fifteen degrees below the horizon: the end of nautical twilight.

Raven alerts and relaxes. I then hear the odd walk of Tad on the path. He sounds a bit like a three-legged animal when in fact he is a four-legged man. Two move as one, and two move awkwardly. I remain still, looking forward to him finding me here.

"Hello."

"Hello."

"Sit."

"Sure."

"You okay?"

"I guess. I left everything behind."

“I know. We took care of it. Raif will FedEx it tomorrow while you’re shopping.”

There is no doubt that I am shopping: another one-day turn-around, another full boat and this time, a six-day trip.

“I think I know better than to ask what’s going on.” This is a fair statement on his part. “But I don’t know what, really, to say, how to start a conversation.”

Calm.

Silence.

Raven drops down on me, putting her nose into my throat. “Yes. You are a good dog. I guess I felt like something ended today while, in fact, all of that changed last year, didn’t it? It was all over last year and the year before. It was over when I left home. It was pretty much over when my mother died.”

“Your mother?”

“Yeah, she’s been my constant thought since I saw the FedEx package. It’s really her that I’m grieving tonight. Odd, huh? I signed a document that put some legal finality to Paul and me. And here comes the ghost of my dead mother, taking the show, the evening, and the event for herself. The one thing she wasn’t in life was selfish. In death, she is rather the opposite. In life, I tried to escape her judgment, to live a life that matched her expectations. In her death, I find she still judges. In her death, she is ever-present. How’s your grandfather?”

“Same, I guess. Older.”

“I’m glad you came home. I think we’d all be dead or in jail if you hadn’t shown up. Things on the old Black Swan were a bit wild there for a bit.”

“And I’d be out an inheritance. I’m certain everything from the boat to the house and land would have been seized.”

"I'm sure of it."

"Are we making money?"

"A little. We're getting by."

"We have passengers."

"Yes, we do."

"And we don't make any money when you're on shore. But I suppose twenty-four hours twice a week is acceptable, huh?"

"Gee, thanks."

What did I want now? "Thaddeus, what do you want now?"

"I don't really know."

"Neither do I." I pet Raven, who is asleep. "It's odd to feel adrift. To let myself go adrift."

"It's all right. The Gulf Stream is just out there. Iceland, Ireland. George's Bank, Virgin Rock, a diminishing number of fishing boats. You'll not get far without company. We're all here too, y'know."

"I know."

16. tunc *tempo: larghetto*

We lay into Finsbay.

Finsbay is a lamb's-eared cove on the island of Cleat. On this dirty day, we groped our way into the cove with radar, depth sounder, and GPS. The weather had been snotty throughout the day. The morning started with a heavy, gray sky and a cold drizzle. The sea to the southwest was black-green, threatening like a weapon. By the forenoon we were soaked by real rain. We sailed through the afternoon, accompanied by heavy rains and a wind that launched spray off the tops of white caps.

To her credit, the Black Swan addressed the afternoon gracefully when let to find the wind on her own. To the regret of all souls aboard, the mate over-steered, causing the schooner to argue with her nature. He further tortured the schooner by carrying too much canvas aloft, creating tension and strain on us all.

Two of my passengers were green. I gave a five-gallon yellow bucket to the more wretched of the two. This he took into an empty stateroom. I could hear his misery through the acid-etched coughing. I encouraged him to get to the deck. It's not a perfect cure. It means puking down into the ocean while getting drenched by a steady, cold rain. Puking in the rain smells better. Additionally, washing requires only that one roll the face skyward. Closed, dark staterooms exacerbate it all.

We passed familiar anchorages during the day, so I took a guess that, at the end of this run, I'd find an orange mooring buoy off our bows.

Bad weather often yielded great speed; this day was no different. Joe and David ran the deck alone. They were capable of doing so. They hoisted the sails together; they tacked the headsails with ease in all conditions. They ran the deck while the mate stood at the helm, spinning the wheel around like a three-year old with a plastic toy. When he tacked, he made a habit of falling off too far, coming through the wind with a jerky motion. Then he had to correct by as much as twenty-five degrees on the new tack. The trail of foam left in his wake tended to describe a serpent, even on his best of days.

I made a light dinner of miso soup and plain rice for the passengers. The boys, I figured, would want something hearty and warm to chew on, so I also roasted a small chicken. It would suffice for Joe, David, and the mate. I counted on the captain not leaving his cabin. I thought he'd be aft with his heroin needle and tiny eyes.

My galley developed a steamy, warm feel to it. The companionway hatch remained closed, trapping the coziness.

I lay below with library books, ignoring the disquieting efforts of the passengers around me. In my way of thinking, this was a fine day to get lazy, to read, and to mind my own thoughts. Let the weather blow, the rain fall. Let the others get cold and wet.

These passengers would not look forward to annual return trips. We treated them so badly. We showed them a miserable, rough time. We drove them to illness instead of cleaving still water in sheltered bays. I wouldn't be surprised if they hit the dock and approached Old Man Abernathy for refunds.

Why did we do this to our passengers? With a little effort, we could have provided each with a small box of scopolamine patches.

This little patch, applied behind an ear, aids prevention of motion sickness. We can find or invent play even on bad days. The net yield would be happy passengers willing to return and recommend us.

After anchoring, I slipped into my foul-weather gear for the first time during the entire day. I opened the sliding hatch over the companionway, leaving the two-foot-high double doors closed. I made a big step over the doors and then pulled the sliding hatch closed.

Water streamed down the rigging in so many spirals. Sails were furled, the booms rested in their crutches. At the end of this wet day, her decks were now clear of crew and mate. As I anticipated, there, off the starboard bow, was an orange mooring buoy. An errant line came over the bow, then made fast at the starboard pin rail. With a tug, I discovered the far end secured the orange mooring buoy to the Black Swan as I had guessed. No doubt, the boys would wait until dark, until they believed all the passengers were well asleep. Then they would slip up here, heaving their sunken booty aboard.

I gave a knowing smile. I may have been blind to this activity at first. Now, their actions had become transparent to me. A true salt would have noted that, although we spent the occasional night next to such mooring buoys, we always anchored. We never moored, thus using the mooring buoy for its apparent intended purpose. We'd anchor directly on top of a mooring buoy. The seasoned sailor would have made the statement to himself: "This is not a mooring buoy." He may have said, "The officers of this schooner have no manners." With either statement, another would have recognized this ruse long before I. The courteous sailor would have left such a mooring buoy ample swing room in case a suitable craft opted to hang on the mooring instead of an anchor. I arrived from Illinois. What did I know of the nuances of nautical courtesy?

The mate took his dinner aft to his cabin. David and Joe ate their chicken and rice wordlessly. The passengers passed a few kind words my way for my thoughtfulness on the dinner selection.

I lay for hours, listening to the night sounds of the Black Swan: rain on the decks, water dripping, people whispering, people sleeping. I was able to see the movement on this boat with my ears. I was able to envision the vigor with which people kept their teeth clean by hearing them brush in the various heads aboard. I heard urine hitting toilet bowls. I heard people fart in the privacy of the head. I heard zippers zipping and unzipping. The sounds registered in the background. I read my book, animating imagines built from the sound-scape.

I rarely heard sounds from the fo'c'sle, a murmur maybe, a boot fall, the sliding of their hatch. I never heard the subtleties of the boy's actions. The bulkhead between us cropped many of the little sounds.

At eleven, according to the watch on the tiny shelf, I heard the stirring I expected: the mate's feet on the sole, the toilet in the aft head getting pumped. From the fo'c'sle, I heard feet shuffle. The after-hatch opened. Footfalls traced a path forward toward the bows. The boys climbed out to the fo'c'sle, one immediately following the other. They pulled their hatch cover closed.

The words were indistinct. The three spoke in hushed tones. But the sound of line on the deck and on the hull was clear. I built a story around the sounds I heard. I imagined the process of hauling contraband up from the bottom of this cove. I worked through the options for hiding drugs under water. First, there would have to be an anchor heavy enough to prevent displacement of the contraband during the ever-cycling tidal currents. They probably used an anchor actually heavy enough to secure pleasure craft. Allowing the mooring buoy to be used to moor boats would lend credence to its disguise. There would have to be enough rake on the line to support the tides in the region. And the drugs, or whatever the contraband was, would be secured underwater. Were they tied to the anchor rode? That didn't make sense because our crew would have to haul the anchor. That is heavy, slow, dirty, and noisy work. Was the contraband available on the anchor rode during low tide? Too risky, others could find the contraband. Two lines from the mooring buoy, one to the mooring, one to the drugs? Again, I fumbled because it would allow others to find the contraband too easily. There had to be a trick to reveal and recover the contraband easily and quietly at night.

The sounds of line on the deck and footfall weren't helping me understand the solution. The hushed tones carried tension. Tension enveloped the mate everywhere. I dismissed this clue, giving further effort to imagining them hauling drugs aboard. I shouldn't care about the process. It shouldn't matter, yet I was more curious about the how-to than the what. I didn't really care what they were smuggling: heroin, cocaine, marijuana, ecstasy, or cash. It would have to be physically small with a high value. *Physically small* would have to be defined as a size that one, two or three people could work from the sea to stowage on the Black Swan with some ease.

How I would answer for myself in a witness chair? It was coming clear to me that I was an accomplice, of a sort, to international smuggling. I was already guilty, probably.

I decided I wanted to understand the darker side of the life into which I had immersed myself. For two months now, I'd kept to my galley. I'd stayed out of the paths of the others, asking only that they afford me the same respect. Tonight, I dressed in long underwear and foul-weather gear. I pulled on my boots. I checked for my waterproof Pelican flashlight, the little rigging knife, and the few bits of safety gear I kept in this jacket.

The smell of my own gear surprised me.

I doused my lights and let my eyes adjust to the near total dark of my galley. I was not blind in this darkness. I suffer no sense of loss in the darkness. I had lived in this small space, night and day, since mid-May. My eyes settled themselves into this black. The pupils opened a bit at a time. The white countertop emerged from the blackness as a fainter shade of black, and the mast became clearer. I stepped toward the companionway.

Do I open my hatch and walk up to them as if this were any other sailing evolution? All parties on deck would know that this really wasn't a standard operation. *They are, in effect, hiding. Walking directly up to them would be a threat, wouldn't it? Do I, instead, lurk in shadows, observing?* With this approach I ran the risk of being discovered. Both methods involved risk. Boldly walking up to the activity, I decided, provided me greater protection, and it allowed me the direct advantage of seeing the technology of smuggling firsthand.

I did want to creep forward partway. I lifted the hatch while I slid it open. I stepped over the doors. I crouched in the darkness after I closed the hatch. My ears informed me that my prey were engaged in hushed but animated conversations at the starboard bow. With temerity, I eased forward.

Shapes resolved: the foremast, bowsprit, and the round buoy, looking like a physical therapy device. Bodies moved in the darkness.

I stepped forward. I envisioned the boys hauling line, but what my eyes saw didn't match expectations. The struggle wasn't with a heavy load coming over the side.

They were not bent over the side, as I anticipated. I saw two silhouettes in one cluster and Joe, taller than both David and the mate, apparently swinging downward, in a clubbing motion. Did he have a belaying pin in his hand? I couldn't tell. I looked above the movement, a trick that helps vision in dim light

Was he giving a killing blow to a flatfish, a flounder they brought up from the bottom? That was illogical. Why would they fish while hauling drugs from the bottom? Was it a fish that got caught accidentally?

I had no sense of depth, just dark shapes against a darker outline. Joe gave another mighty swing downward, his arm and the belaying pin contrasting against the night sky.

I took steps forward; temerity ebbed, timidity flooded. I felt no real fear, just confusion. I couldn't reconcile the images with my expectations. My ears yielded nothing to abate the confusion. I couldn't see well enough to identify details. People moved with the flatness of shadow puppets. A scene cut of black paper on a dark gray background: shapes moving, arms swinging, and the Black Swan's bulwarks. Without depth and color, my sight abstracted the scene beyond recognition.

I heard the distinct sound of a crunch, like gravel grinding below a footfall.

Joe mumbled to David. I heard David gasping. He was gulping for air. I sensed him to be in trouble, probably from that damn mate again. I made the last steps forward.

"David?"

He didn't respond.

Both of the boys were silent, I felt their agitation and surprise.

"Are you guys okay?"

I started to understand that the mate lay on the deck. I wasn't entirely sure. "What's he doing down there."

He was silent. "Is he going to be all right?" They still hadn't answered my questions. David breathed: in and out, in and out. The gulping nature of his breaths dissipated. His panic subsided a degree.

Why was it always David that got hurt? Did the fucking mate just thrive on perceived weakness? I decided that, even if these guys didn't press charges, I would talk to Dale, the police chief. If I couldn't get the mate arrested for assault, then I could at least get him fired, if for no other reason than fostering a hostile environment. Of all the times I had been in meetings when people discussed hostile environments, never once did I think I'd have to deal with bloody violence.

The mate lay quietly, the quick beaten from him. I was glad for that. We got David seated on the fo'c'sle hatch cover.

"Joe?"

He mumbled a response. After two months, I still didn't understand him. I wanted to shake him and shout, with great clarity in my voice, "Speak so I can hear you." I spoke; my frustration had been building since I met the boy. "Joe, I can't understand you. You've got to speak up."

"I think I hit him too hard." I understood him, finally.

We stepped to the mate. I bent down, dropping to a knee. He was still, posed like a sleeping person on his side, one cheek on the deck. Rain sluiced down the contours of his face. Was his eye open?

"Joe? I'm going to turn on my flashlight."

He mumbled again while handing me his flashlight. His shone red. I understood his statement: Joe had said, "Mine's red."

I returned the white light to my pocket.

The mate's one eye was open. Blood, I thought, looks black in red light. There wasn't much blood. But there was a ton of rain, rain on a sloping deck, a deck designed to shed water, shed water and blood, apparently.

Calmly, I developed the belief that this mate, Samuel Selby, had died. I rolled him to his back. There, sticking through his slicker, stood the handle of a rigging knife. I used my thumb and fingers on the mate's neck to find a pulse. I didn't have a clue, given I had only been trained by TV shows. I stuck my thumb into my own neck to find my pulse, using my neck as a map to the mate's neck. I didn't find anything that resembled a pulse.

I had rolled him to his back and now saw that both eyes were open. His full face was exposed and looking toward the dark night. I moved the red light across his eyeballs. These pupils were non-reactive. They did nothing in the light.

"Joe, come 'ere." I spoke softly. He looked at me and bent down. "Sorry." I apologized for the pass of the red light over his eyeballs. His pupils contracted as the light became more intense. I did the same, again, to the mate. The eyeballs remained fixed, the pupils, unchanged.

"I think he's dead."

By then, Joe had seen the knife.

I stood.

Poor David was still having a difficult time. I put my hand to the small of his back. His sheath knife was not where it belonged. The sheath was there, but empty.

I comforted David while sitting with him. I replayed the puppet show of shapes. I filled in the gaps. The evidence lay about me, evidence like Lego blocks strewn about the deck, awaiting assembly. I had to snap the shapes, the sounds, and the missing pieces together to construct the events in three dimensions.

Joe pulled the knife from the mate's body. He opened the mate's slicker and grabbed a hunk of shirt. He used this shirt-end to wash David's knife. He wet the knife on the slicker, scrubbed it, and dried it with the shirt. When he was done, he put the knife back into David's sheath.

He repeated the same methodical cleaning process for the belaying pin. He wet it in shallow puddles that pooled on the mate's jacket. Then he wiped it clean with the shirt. When he was done, he re-buttoned the mate's shirt and closed the jacket. I held the red light, still on. I sat with an arm around David, watching Joe's evolutions.

I recognized the many things now required: cops, lawyers, the Coast Guard, dealing with Paul, interviews with Dale Abernathy. I'd witnessed a murder. No, I hadn't. I'd witnessed a death. This was self-defense. The mate was trying to kill David by choking him.

I shut all this off. I tried, anyway.

Someone had to tell the captain.

I stood from the hatch cover. I made a step aft. I felt Joe's hand on my wrist. His grip was firm but not demanding, not threatening. He spoke. Of course, I didn't understand him. Annoyed with his mumbling, I wiggled my arm free.

He mumbled on and grabbed again. I used my other hand to push him away. *He's a liability in a crisis.* I walked back toward the aft-hatch. I slid the top open, stepped over the doors, and climbed down. This was my first time down this companionway, first time in two months, first time since joining this forsaken crew.

The smaller port-side stateroom was the mate's. I knew this from both observing the traffic while on deck and hearing the movements during the last months.

At the starboard stateroom door, I gave a polite rap.

"Captain," I said in a soft voice. "Captain?"

I rapped again. "Captain."

I opened the door and directed Joe's red flashlight around the room. The captain lay in a large and comfortable bunk. His room was very nearly clean. Articles all had been stowed. I made my way to him. "Captain, we need you on deck." I shook him.

He stirred but didn't really wake. "Captain."

I was looking at my second set of dead but open eyes for the night. The captain was warm. I did the thumb-and-fingers in the throat thing again. This time there was a pulse. I pulled down his bed sheets, thinking I could assist him to his feet.

Thankfully, he was dressed in a loose pair of boxer shorts. I scanned his body. His navel was a deep, nasty color. I couldn't accurately judge the color under Joe's red light. It looked black — blood in his navel. .

I scanned the space around us. And just like in the movies, I found a spoon, a hypodermic needle, a lighter, and a vial. Paul had been right: my captain was a heroin addict. He was probably right about the hepatitis as well.

I didn't try to speak to him again.

I covered this useless captain, tempted to cover his face as if he too were dead.

Joe had been right too. Clearly, he knew.

It was my time to discover my world, my world of a heroin-addicted boss and a violent, now murdered, first mate, and my world of drug smuggling. My response was one of resolution, resolution, coming in the form of clarity, and understanding. Resolution, like a picture came into focus. My world resolved into an interconnected, complex picture.

I heard movement forward. The boys had taken steps. They opened their hatch. They moved about the forepeak and the deck. I closed the stateroom door behind me. On deck, seventy feet now separated me from the boys forward. I walked a purposeful stride.

David had recovered enough to help Joe. Joe seemed to be dragging the mate aft. David struggled under a separate load. I stopped. Joe had the mate by the feet, dragging him, one leg per side, dragging the mate as if he were dragging a wheelbarrow.

I joined them at the taffrail. David carried a pile of chain. He struggled to place the chain silently on the deck. Joe removed seizing wire and snips from a pocket. Joe took one wind of chain around the mate's waist, and then he used a length of seizing wire to make a tight-fitting belt.

"No!" I whispered. "No, you can't do that. This is a crime scene. You guys will be all right. It was self-defense. I'll testify to that."

Joe and David worked together silently, feeding chain through his crotch, up to his neck, around his neck, and down around a leg again. They did another wind on the waist, then another wind along the length of the torso. At many of the intersections, they used seizing wire to bind the chain to itself. "Come on guys, you can't do this."

They did not listen.

"This doesn't solve any problems. We still have to arrive in port with a missing mate, don't we? We can't just explain away the disappearance of a member of our crew to our passengers." They finished trussing the mate.

"We still have to call the Coast Guard. We can't get home from here. Don't we need the mate? Don't we need to report this, somehow?" Now I sounded ridiculous. Was I more guilty because I saw all this? Was I more guilty now than I was when I hid in my galley? Was I actually innocent? There isn't really a 911 service out here. I could have used the radio to call the Coasties in. I had never used the radio and didn't have a lick of training on it. But a few "Maydays" yelled into the mic, and people would understand.

When the boys bent to pick up the mate, I turned on my white light. "Please," I whispered, "don't do this." I stood, putting my hand on Joe's shoulder. He mumbled something back to me. They rested the mate on the cap rail. Joe spoke to David. David both understood and nodded. They took the mate's arms while working to push his legs over the side. They got him vertical and lowered him to the extent of their reach. I was at the rail with them now. My white light shone on the mate's head when they let go.

The head rocked back while he sunk. The eyes tilted toward the black sky one last time. The seawater turned his dead face green.

Ghost-like, he faded from sight.

I watched the empty space in the water. Tiny bubbles returned to the surface, little pockets of air trapped within his clothing. I saw a larger complex of bubbles rising through the green. They burst and foamed at the surface, one last exhale from dead lungs.

I felt relief. "Good riddance, asshole." Relief mixed with an understanding of the eventual consequences. I don't know if I said that out loud. I'd be horrified with myself, if I actually did.

The boys were returning forward to the fo'c'sle.

"No." I barked in a hushed whisper. "No, we're going to discuss this." I had just decided that I was in charge, me, the former corporate executive. I was not going to let two idiots ruin my life. I wasn't going to go to jail over their hairbrained actions. They both turned around. Joe beckoned.

We climbed down into the fo'c'sle. Joe turned on D.C.-powered electric lights. Our eyes adjusted while we dropped out of our foul-weather gear. Joe mumbled something to David. I still didn't understand.

Dressed only in my long underwear, I sat on a clean bunk, "Damn it, Joe. I need to understand you. Can you, just for tonight, speak up and talk a little slower for me. Shit, I feel like I'm deaf when I am around you."

David answered. "Even an accidental death during the commission of a felony is murder one."

"So what. It's all in how you spin it. You could have been preventing the felony. What's the felony anyway? Smuggling? No one has to know that you were smuggling. If there's no smuggling, then there's no felony."

Joe bent forward and opened a drawer below my feet. I lifted my feet and looked down. It was full of sealed packages, stuff wrapped in plastic and taped. "There's more."

"Oh."

"We've got it hidden throughout the fo'c'sle and the chain locker. We can't be boarded."

"What is it?" I couldn't tell heroin from coke or cakes of baking soda. My question remained unanswered.

I guessed smuggling also meant that I had been transporting drugs for two months, that I had been feeding guys who transported and handled drugs. *Oh. It does rule out the US Coast Guard.* "What if it all went to the bottom again?"

"It won't fit in tonight's container. We could sink it, but . . . "

"But what? That makes more sense doesn't it? Sink the drugs and deal with the Coast Guard and cops on the mate's accidental death. It was self-defense."

"Too much risk. They'd find us and pro'ly kill us. No."

"Who'd kill you?" It was a stupid question, but it only sounded stupid after I said it. David didn't answer.

Joe spoke. It sounded a lot like, "He just disappeared. Stormy sea."

Then David finished, " . . . and he went over. We anchored."

"No, the passengers saw him get his dinner."

"He just disappeared in the night. We don't know what happened to him. Maybe he stepped off the transom, drunk? Maybe it was suicide? It could just be a mystery."

I wended my way through complex tales of disaster. My mind was trying to answer all the questions that may get asked of us. I worked at spinning a complex story into which the disappearance of the mate easily fit.

David addressed me: "Maggie, you were in the galley all night, asleep. You don't know anything. Don't worry about it."

Joe spoke in a way that only David understood him, again.

"We've both been in jail, several times. Simple is best. There is no evidence. There is no body. The cops can get all wound up about this if they want. They can look at us all day long if that's what they want. You were asleep. Joe and I walked the deck at midnight to check the anchor and the weather. We saw nothing and went back to our racks. If passengers think they heard something, it was us making our rounds and securing the boat during a dirty night. Tomorrow, we wake up and start the day. When we can't find the mate, we're all surprised. We look and . . . "

"And what? We just sail home without him?"

"Yes."

"We don't call the Coast Guard? We don't call the cops?"

"Nope. We get home as if all is normal. We see the passengers off. We off-load. Then we wander to the police station to report his disappearance."

"It won't work."

"It's either that or Joe and I get dead or get chased around for the rest of our lives. We'd rather take our chances with the small town cops."

Joe and David both stood up, clearly my signal to leave. I put on my wet gear and climbed from their fo'c'sle back to the deck. From there, I returned to my galley for a poor night's rest.

David came into the galley while I was serving oatmeal. The passengers' minds and their stomachs remembered the insults of the sea. Oatmeal was another kindness I could offer. I knew of the day to follow, the pounding run home. The rain and the wind hadn't abated. While we slept and ate in the quiet of Finsbay, the passengers were contented. Oatmeal is soothing and gentle going down. Furthermore, it is not horrible coming back up. I encouraged drinking water.

David had a shocked and somewhat panicked look upon his face when he appeared on my companionway. I mirrored his shock, thinking that things had actually just gotten worse. I wasn't acting. I feared it all getting worse. Maybe the mate rose from the bottom, or the Coasties awaited us at the opening of the cove or maybe the captain killed himself with an overdose during the night. The situation looked bad enough that I didn't want to alarm my passengers.

I pulled David away from the table. I pulled him toward my bunk and the galley head. "What's up? You look very upset. What's wrong?" I said all of this in a hushed and hurried tone.

He responded in a louder and clearer voice than was necessary. "We can't find the mate."

Oh, shit. I was playing a role. "What do you mean the mate is missing?" I stuck with the hushed tones.

"He's not in his stateroom, and we can't find him on board." Obviously, he wanted the passengers to overhear bits of the conversation.

"Well, he's got to be here." I didn't have a script. I played the scene as if this news were new and as if this news were the truth. "You just don't disappear." I kept my voice low and my tone concerned. I didn't really want anyone to remember me in this play.

In full voice, I said to the folks gathered at my table, "I'll be right back." I pulled on my still-wet slicker and sou'wester.

"You're stickin' with this stupid idea?"

"Trust us."

Shit. There wasn't any way I could trust these two. I didn't know them. And trusting them shouldn't have been the issue. I was the witness. I was the witness to the felonies. I was the witness to the murder. I was the witness to the disposal of the body and thus, the evidence. "I take it I am now helping you look for the mate?"

"You do what you want. Just tell the world you slept through the night. And tell what you see this morning." I walked with David down to the mate's quarters.

Joe was in the captain's quarters, trying to get the captain on his feet, alert, and ready to head to the dock. One way or the other, the captain was also going to have to speak with the police. What would his story be? — that he was asleep in his quarters all night?

David and I acted out the process of me stepping into the shit-hole of a stateroom that the mate lived in. We gave a solid look in all the spaces large enough to conceal a man-sized object. With just a bit of sarcasm, I said, "Gee, David, he's not in here."

"No, he's not."

"You've checked the fo'c'sle?" *Why not play it through for the non-existent audience.*

"Yes."

"Well, I'll check all the staterooms. Maybe he fell or something in an empty stateroom." And with that said, I actually climbed up to the deck and headed toward the galley. I made an effort to look for the mate in all the rooms, empty or not.

I realized that what I said to the passengers didn't matter a lot. There was an expectation that I spin the truth to assure them of their safety. It's like being on an airplane with engine problems. The passengers don't expect the entire truth. I only had to meet their expectations with a statement that would assure them of their safe return home.

I stepped back into the galley. The passengers had a sense of mishap. They were attuned to the movements, the tone, and the words of the crew.

"There is nothing to be concerned about. Our first mate, Samuel Selby, seems to be missing from the schooner. There is a search going on now. We don't think that any foul play has been involved. We'll probably spend a little while taking an assessment of our next actions. Our priority of the day will be getting all of you safely back to the dock. One of the crew members or the captain will keep you informed as this develops." As if the captain would be able to speak a word to these people.

David and Joe made a show of inflating the folding Zodiac and rowing it to the shore of the island. An hour later, they rowed back. At eleven, the captain made a few appearances on deck. I informed the passengers that we would sail for home, "with all possible speed." David made a brief announcement to the assembly that radio calls had been made to the Coast Guard, alerting them of a man-overboard at our location, Milovaig Island.

The name rang in my head. We were at Cleat Island, not Milovaig. I knew both islands.

I pulled recollections of the last day. I asked myself if I had ever previously mentioned our location to any of the passengers. The passengers were all too sick to spend time on deck, too sick to be inquisitive. Maybe the more current information would superimpose the older information.

I followed David to the deck. "How can you do that? How can you change our location?"

"We have to. That's what's in the log. The mate wrote that last night in pen, along with his notation about the anchorage and weather. If he wrote that we were anchored in Milovaig, then clearly, that's where we have to be. That's where the passengers have to know us to be. And we have to talk about being at Milovaig. We have to remember being there."

I reviewed again: the passengers never spent more than a few minutes on deck. Even if they had, the lousy weather would have changed the shape of the land, the sea, and the sky. One miserable cove would look very like another. They could each probably return here and not recognize it. They could get taken to Milovaig Island and really not know the difference.

I took the helm while the boys hoisted the staysails and finished hauling the anchor. With the anchor catted home, I rounded out into the Gulf of Maine. Joe came to my side and pointed to another sylvan island directly on our nose. I actually heard and understood him to say, "Sail there, that's Milovaig."

They hoisted a double-reefed main while leaving the fore furled. They hoisted the jib as well. Under reduced sail, the boat moved happily. One of these two knew how to sail and sailed well. I didn't know which. Joe ducked into the aft companionway again. Clearly, his duty was to keep the captain free and clear of his own habits. It's one thing to be a tonic to oneself when nobody cares. Today, or tonight, whenever we arrived home, there would be some scrutiny. We needed an alert captain.

During an extended shift at the helm, I sailed a partial circuit around Milovaig. David joined me at the helm. He turned on the marine radio and started a call:

"Pahn-pahn, pahn-pahn, pahn-pahn. This is the schooner Black Swan calling on marine radio channel sixteen. We are reporting the loss of our first mate overboard at or around the vicinity of Milovaig Island. This incident occurred during the hours after midnight on the fifteenth of July. Break." David took a breath before continuing in a slow, clear tone. He was making the call that he had already told the passengers he made.

Thus began the narrative with the officials. During the communication, David professionally identified our location, our destination, and the number of souls aboard. He marched through a clearly scripted dialogue.

I served soup from cans with a basket of pilot bread for the passengers. It was the worst meal I'd served since joining this crew. The choices I had were limited. I needed to be on the deck during every evolution. Joe and David had to share the duties of the rigging. We three recognized that I didn't have the strength nor the skills that the boys had at tacking and sail trim. Therefore, I took the mate's place at the wheel.

The attitude of the day relaxed. I found myself enjoying the helm. The weather followed my lead. As I calmed, so did the sea. As I brightened, so did the sky. It would be a late evening of sailing. I would have to find a way to prepare all of our meals. *Roasting meat doesn't take much time.* I decided I could do bits of cooking between maneuvers.

Joe came to me at the helm. He leaned in. "You're doin' good." I heard him. I actually heard him.

I peeked behind. My foamy wake was sharp and razor straight.

17. nunc *tempo: andante*

I step into BATS at 8:00 PM. That's late for me, but my restocking follows the tides, and the tides follow the moon. I arrive at Ralph's just as the sun is starting to dip into the west.

"Twenty minutes to sunset," I announce to the crew. "Raif, how about that po' boy of yours and a beer? That would set me right. What a glorious day!"

I am not the center of attention. Nor am I the topic of conversation, just a latecomer to dinner. I sit and listen to the conversation they are having. Stuart is telling a tale of one of his years in college. David, Joe, Kieran, and Tad are all absorbed in the accents and animation Stuart uses to bring the tale to life. Tad's cousin, Dale is seated with our crew. Ralph leans on a chair. He's enjoying the story too.

I now feel guilty asking for food while he is so entertained. I hold my hand up, telling him to slow down, to stop. I am too late to catch the story. Instead, I watch my crew, my happy little crew. I reset my hand on Kieran's near-side shoulder, dropping my forearm down his back. I lean forward in my chair and listen. I look across the table at Tad, wanting his eyes to find mine.

Stuart's telling manifests images, characters, and places. I lose track of my crew, getting absorbed into Stuart's world. There are bits about extracted DNA looking rather like camel snot, lab fridges with chilled Oreos and Petri dishes, and a professor proving time after time that there are no facts. The professor calls out challenges to his freshmen students: "Give me a fact. Give me an indisputable fact." In his time, the professor—through Stuart—gives illustrations where two plus two is not four. Facts fail. With wit and humility, Stuart tosses great facts to the wind.

Ralph has taken a seat before Stuart finishes his yarn, his deconstructionist creation myth.

Ralph stands. "Newtonian physics and quantum mechanics . . . I'll get Maggie's sandwich."

I feel obliged to wait for Ralph's reappearance, letting the conversation flow. I detach from myself, joining the flow of those who now surround me. Kieran starts another of his goofy Irish stories that he seems to change to fit each occasion.

I eat.

I listen.

Nine o'clock passes. "It's gettin' late for me, boys. I'm going to head to my bunk after an announcement. I am going to buy a house here." It has only been a few weeks since the finalization of the divorce. I signed the papers at this very table.

"Which one?" Ralph asks.

"I don't know."

"Is it going to be around here?"

"Well, yeah. That's the purpose of my announcement. I am buying a house here."

Their non-response hits me as if they are all mumbling, "So what?" I don't know what they are thinking, but this is big news for me. I trust Kieran to see my thoughts first. He tunes quickly to people. That empathy is the source of his kindness.

"Mags, how do you think that this can be news to us? Did you think that anyone at this table or in this village was thinking you were going to pull out with the next tide? You're building a bloody huge boat." He puts his arm around me, giving a hug. "I'd rather think this town would build you a house if you wanted them to."

"Oh, stop it. You're full of it."

"No Maggie, you're full of it."

"I do have news. Real news." Tad interrupts my willingness to give childish sparring to Kieran.

"Yes?"

"Just kidding, I don't really have any news. Except I just now started thinking about selling ten acres. I think we should schedule a field trip. We should all go see how the Raven is doing in the shipyard. The launching of our new schooner is only weeks away. With the winter to fit her, we'll be ready for a few shake downs by late spring."

Our coastal schooner empire is doubling in size. Tad and I spent a year discussing the marketing and business opportunities for a second schooner, a vessel we have named after the original Black Swan's twin sister. We decided that, with the right planning, we could haul kayaks. We could sail across big water and let people paddle in the evenings and around the quieter water. In moments of silliness, we decided to continue smuggling, albeit legally, for the most part. Although we are a great distance from Boston, the de facto capital of New England, we are a great deal closer to Canada than the other schooner ports. We could become a regular, annual means for people to get to Nova Scotia and Grand Manan Island for prescriptions, decent toilets, good beer, and shower heads that move more water than air.

Regardless of the real opportunities, I wanted to recreate the environment of having two identical schooners: the Raven and the Black Swan. We have asked Lyttle Shipyard to trick the new schooner as the old one was. Of course, we have a pile of new Coast Guard rules to oblige, rules so complicated that we quickly discovered you can't build an old-fashioned boat during this century. I argued that we ought to capitalize on the shady smuggling past of these old girls.

I envision ads reading: "Come sail the Coast of Maine on the Smuggling Schooner Black Swan. Ply the coast, concealed in the dark of night." We can no longer thumb our noses at the US Coast Guard, INS, Maine State Police, the Canadian Coast Guard, and others who now patrol these waters with every manner of surveillance technology. We may not literally tweak these officials, but we can play. We can let others play.

We have also gone to a local fellow to make us a pair of matching launches. We had their names long before we had the sense to make new boats. One shall be Signet, the other, Fledge. The youth of our fleet.

How many at this table share the secret about the Mate? How many at this table know the truth? How many in the village know the truth? And who among us has guessed at it? Nobody has ever spoken of that night since. Each in his way is a tacit accomplice; each knows that to address that night is to acknowledge our separate roles. I can only surmise that our police chief, Dale, would far rather have the mate gone and the family safe.

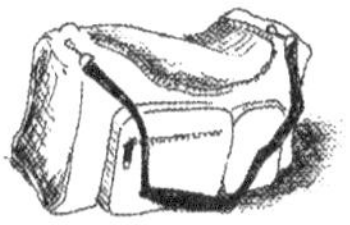

18. tunc *tempo: vivo*

Passengers fled.

As soon as they woke, they dashed. We'd arrived too late for any to find a hotel. Furthermore, given that we arrived at the very trough of a low tide, we had them trapped aboard for one more horrible night.

It took Dale Abernathy a short while to round them up the next morning. He found every one of them. He sat us all in the selectmen's meeting room. To each, he asked the same group of questions.

I waited and waited.

The officer at the police desk got calls from Dale. He'd go to the conference room and take another passenger upstairs. When couples reunited, they left without another look.

The captain got called upstairs.

Joe got called upstairs. And I waited.

David got called upstairs. And I waited.

David was released, and I still waited.

He came down to get me himself.

I worked like hell to read him. I tried to assess his body language, his eyes, and his gestures. First, I recognized that I had never read him well. Second, I realized he was firm in not communicating. He was effective at not communicating. I admired this trait in him. His stock rose while we walked upstairs.

"Have a nice sail?" That was his first question after I sat down.

"No. Not really."

"Humm. Wanna know what I heard?"

"Sure . . . ?"

"Everyone went to bed. They all slept. David and Joe check the anchor and the deck around midnight. The gent in cabin one and the gent in cabin four heard some vague noise around that time. During breakfast, David came in. You were very shocked to hear that the mate was missing. You went off to look for him. You were reported to have poked in every cabin before returning to the galley. David and Joe each tell me that you were asleep through the night.

"Apparently, you got to bed early and rose around 4:30.

"The mate was seen at dinner and never again. Is that correct?"

"Yes." I hoped that my face expressed more of a surprised look than anything. "And?"

"And nothing. Did you sleep through the night?"

"Pretty much. I heard the boys check the deck, but that was it. I can hear people use the head during the night, but it was quiet. It was just another night on the Black Swan."

"Okay, then let's go through the story once. You tell me what you saw and heard. Start with dinner. Tell me the details, who ate what. Tell me snippets of the conversations. Relive the night."

I did. Detail after detail, I told him how I could hear at night, how I built images of the boat in the water and peoples' muted nighttime activities. I told him about seasickness, yellow buckets. I talked about my regret that we don't keep Dramamine or scopolamine for the passengers. I talked about my frustration that we didn't keep inland, sailing the sheltered waters that the coast had to offer. I described lighting my stove.

I described the first time I entered the mate's quarters. Here, Dale asked questions. He drove harder on the details. He drove harder on my experiences. He forced me to admit that I had never previously been down the aft companionway. I fought having to tell him this. I didn't want to admit this out loud. I got defiant with the information once I did. "No, of course I hadn't been down there. I never got invited, and there was nothing down there for me . . . "

I described the deck as it appeared in the morning. I described the stateroom. I often closed my eyes. At times, I rolled my eyes to the left, envisioning my movements that morning. When Dale asked about my emotional state, I evaded. I offered words like "shock," "incredulous."

"Well, the passengers say that you looked annoyed and impatient."

"I probably was. They are such idiots. I haven't a clue what I am doing here with these people. I don't belong here."

"That's your call, Margaret. You can leave anytime. You chose to stay. What's more, people like your food. And they appreciate what you do for them when you are sailing. In fact, talking about you was the closest the passengers came to a compliment about their entire trip. When this is over, I have a lot more questions for you on another topic."

"Like what?"

"Like, what the hell were you guys doing out there? Why go to Milovaig or wherever you were? I'll need to know about the smuggling at some point, very soon. Tell the boys with that fucking mate gone or dead, it's over. I have called my cousin, Tad. He is going to come home and take over. Uncle Isaac is too old, and he's lost track of what this modern world is about. Do you understand my message?"

There was little doubt what his message was.

"I've told the boys that I will be down there this afternoon with the state police. We're going to investigate the disappearance of Selby. They should get here around two, and we'll be down there shortly there after." He looked out the window toward the schooner.

I walked straight toward David and Joe upon leaving the town hall. They were unloading green trash bags from the schooner to the back of a tiny Nissan pickup truck.

I watched. They made two trips.

David gave a little shout. "We're off to the landfill."

"What about the captain and his quarters? Did you clean that as well?"

"Yes."

I thought I ought to go pack my kit. The season was over. This career was over. And the government was about to seize the schooner. I walked toward the dock, neither wanting to stay nor wanting to go. I had little to do and nowhere to go. Jail for smuggling had little appeal. For that matter, neither did the legal ramifications of covering up a murder or a death, whichever that was. I stepped toward the lip of the dock, put my hands out, grabbed a shroud, and swung down to the railing. Child's play. I was climbing on a jungle gym and swinging on rope toys. Yet the playfulness had gone. Gone to corruption, rotted and putrefied with long abuse.

Instead of descending to my galley, I climbed. I took the ratlines up the mast. Hands gripping shrouds, feet on small black line, I climbed: hand over hand, foot over foot. At the top of the main mast,

I clung. At the topmast, the top of the main mast, sundry terminals for stays and shrouds crowded. I could see the road leading west, the direction from which I had come. I could see the islands that dotted the coast. I could see the tight boundaries of the small village and the community that surrounded it. I could see my own car parked by the two empty dumpsters on the west side of the parking lot. There were no mysteries revealed from this height.

I did wonder at the ability of old-time sailors to slide down line. I pictured Errol Flynn breaking a fall with a knife stuck through a sail, gliding gently down the belly of a great square sail with a hand on a knife. No decent sailor would do that to a sail, and no student of physics would accept the process.

I climbed down. I found getting down harder than I expected. My hands were picking up the black pitch; my feet swung in the little steps. I had run and running got me here. Running had made so little sense, but finding this out at the land's end, didn't serve. I didn't have a place to go. I didn't have a soul that needed me. The song of freedom can be a lament, if you view freedom as a loss of connection. A tall mast is an easy place to have such thoughts. I kept climbing down: foot, foot, hand, hand; foot, foot, hand, hand.

I went to my galley, so unlike those first days. Each device, now, had a home. Cast-iron skillets and pans replaced the aluminum. White surfaces were white. The sink was clean. A faint odor of lemon bleach remained.

I reminded myself of the first days on board, of the microwave that sat there, the rotted food in the iceboxes. I remembered my horror while I cleaned, the turning of my stomach while I discovered moulds and rot.

I packed. I folded my clothing neatly. I balled my socks neatly. I rolled my underwear neatly. I pressed them into the duffle bags. I lined my sea boots up next to my sneakers and the pairs of sandals I had. I left my foul-weather gear on the stout, wooden hangers I bought. I hung them from the upper bunk. I took my anorak off its hanger. I folded my heavy wool sweater after sniffing it. I buried my nose in lanolin, the trapped sea spray, and the smell of mist. My entire summer, I saw, would fit easily back into the small trunk of my car.

I carried the bags to the deck. I laid them neatly on the starboard side. Tide had dropped farther. The deck hung about ten feet below the dock. With the next trip, I draped the foul-weather gear on the rail. With the third trip, I carried a trash bag of footwear. I reclined over the companionway hatch. The rigging seemed to move through the gray/ yellow/ green/ white clouds. And there I lay, waiting for the moon to move. When the moon moved, the tides here would swell. The deck would return to the level of the dock, and I could disembark with a bit of grace. I shut my eyes.

"Ahoy, the Black Swan." There was a lilt of a brogue in the address. I sat up. "Oh hello, is the captain aboard."

"No." I didn't know if we still had a captain. I didn't know if he was on board, but nobody would want to see our captain.

"Permission to come aboard?"

"Sure, come on down."

He leapt out a shroud and spun down it like a pro. "Name's Kieran Brogan. I hear that there might be a job opening for a licensed deck officer."

"I guess so. We had one disappear at sea."

"That's what I heard. So, who do I talk to?"

"I don't really know. I was thinking of heading out. I am Margaret Noonan. I have been the cook since May. You might try the town cop, well, actually top cop. Dale Abernathy is the owner's grand-nephew. He'll probably be in the town hall. Ask for Chief Abernathy."

"No shit, really. Huh? Well, Margaret Noonan, it was a pleasure meeting you."

"You have your license?"

"Yup. US Coast Guard Hundred Ton Master, Oceans, with sailing endorsement."

"And the lilt, that's not from South Boston, is it?"

"Nope, Mayo. Born and raised, thanks be to God. But I did happen to have a Yank for a father."

"Not bad."

"Wanna show me around a bit?"

"Sure. Dale will be around in a while. He's bringing the state troopers."

I gave him a tour of the schooner, which consisted of a tour of the deck and a tour of my galley. I avoided both the aft staterooms and the fo'c'sle. When it came to giving the tour to a licensed captain, the effort became rather trivial. With passengers, every line is a mystery. The processes are new. Life at sea is a different life than the one lived on land. Kieran put his hand on my countertops, and he looked at my bunk space.

He peeked in my icebox. It was empty, save one large box of open baking soda.

"Looks like you're closed."

"I think my job is over."

"Well, if your job is over, then I certainly don't have one, do I?"

"I don't really know. There are probably bookings through the rest of the summer. We're supposed to sail into October."

"Then we'd need a cook, don't ya think?"

"Oh, I just took a little sabbatical from work to goof off for the summer. This isn't what I do."

“Not what I’ve heard around town. I hear about your cooking all over the place. You keep this operation together is what I hear.”

“I should get home. There’s a house, a husband, a job, and the rest of the life back there.”

“Back where?”

“Illinois.”

“Nah, you don’t want to go back, do ya? What kind of a job do you have anyway? Flippin’ steaks at some haughty restaurant? This is funner.”

“No, I’m a vice president for a very large telecommunications company.” It was a line I hadn’t actually used for months.

“They’re not missing you, are they?”

“Dale will be down shortly. We can wait on deck.” I ignored his comment.

The tide slowly brought the schooner back to the dock, a slow elevator rising and lowering about thirty inches per hour.

“What else have you heard about this boat?”

“A little of this and that, I guess.”

“If you were the mate, would we continue pursuing ‘this and that,’ as it were?”

“That’s not my call. I don’t even know if the rumors are true.”

“They’re true.”

“Oh.” He genuinely sounded disappointed. “Why hasn’t anything been done.”

“I think something is about to be done.”

“Is that why you’re leaving?”

“No. Of course not.”

"Is that why you stayed?"

"No. I had nothing to do with all that. I think it was Selby, the mate that was responsible."

"Then it's over?"

"If the family has anything to do with it, then yes, I'd say so. I think Selby ran his own little drug running operation under the noses of the family and the passengers for years. If I had to guess, he fed the Abernathy bogus passenger fees with some of his proceeds. He kept the captain in a captive state of drug use and ran this schooner like his own little fiefdom."

"So you lived through it, and that's over, right? So why go?"

"Because I should. It was stupid of me to come here. I came here chasing some damned lost-youth idea. I came here to rediscover the smells of my father's sweaters and the adventures my uncles discussed with hushed tones. I came here to find home, and I just landed in some ridiculous facsimile of life everywhere." My mother had left this coast after my father was lost at sea.

She and her sister dragged me to Illinois. There, in my plaid skirt and white blouse of a Catholic school, my language separated me from my peers. I carried the color of nautical language from this shore to a brick and limestone building on the edge of a small lake. I parroted the stories I heard from the men when they sat in the parlor smoking. I hadn't a clue what they meant. I understood neither the stories nor the specifics of the words I used. The punishments I took were punishments for my mother, for pulling me from my home, for putting me in a school with nuns for teachers. In those first months, I was quick to draw a crowd. Later, I learned to blend with the new surroundings.

I lost flavor of the language and the accent. The stories shortly lost their credibility. Throughout my life, I sought the older, softer speech of this coast. I expected to find men still dressed in checkered, woolen shirts, men sitting with pipes laughing at those who chased them, laughing with others who told of shooting rifles to protect lobster pots, men laughing at their own idiocy in the face of green water over their bows, men retelling stories in which selectmen and clergy helped hide the bounty of foreign wrecks. In these stories, anyone official, federal, or from away was the enemy, and brotherhood was found among the men of the coastal trades. They told and retold secrets on the porches of friends, secrets forever denied beyond these narrow borders. I carried these stories from Maine to Illinois, telling them with abandon. Without the sea, islands, international waters, and fishing boats, these stories sounded like the fiction of a child's mind.

"Would you mind if I poke around the aft staterooms?"

"No, why would I mind? Just don't touch anything. The state police are on their way down. You probably don't want fingerprints where you can't explain them, do you?"

"I'll just tell them the truth." I liked his arrogance.

Kieran Brogan bounded aft. I lay back down, trying not to care about his efforts and his opinion of this schooner. We were still a couple of feet below the dock when two o'clock struck at the Presbyterian church. The dock remained quiet. I heard neither cars nor people. We were close enough to the dock to afford a graceful departure, yet I remained. Kieran had returned to the deck. He now explored the rigging.

At 2:30, I picked up my larger duffle bag and the shopping bag of shoes. Kieran offered to help. I told him to keep exploring. Walking slowly to my car, I watched a man hop down from a van. He put one arm in a crutch, then the other. I looked at him long enough so I gave the impression of not looking away. He walked toward me. Actually, he walked toward my car. When I understood that it was his intent to meet me, I watched him. He moved in an easily swinging manner.

"Margaret?"

"Yes. Margaret Noonan." I held my hand back. It seemed inappropriate to offer my hand.

"I am Tad Abernathy." He stuck his hand out to me. The crutch hung from his forearm. We shook hands, and I felt massive calluses on his palm, calluses formed by the Tflike handle. "We've met once before, haven't we? I believe it was your first day here."

"It was, wasn't it?"

"You're not leaving are you?"

"I think so." *Tad Abernathy will be the bookends of my adventures on the coast of Maine.*

"Please don't. I'd like you to stay." He smiled. His teeth were immaculate. His green eyes had little flecks of golden yellow. "What do I need to do to convince you to hang around for a little while longer?"

"I don't know."

He said the words Paul never said. He said the words the assholes on the Executive Management Team said but never meant. I paused a moment, enjoying his warmth. "I'll give you through September if you do two things: first, hire the Irish kid over there as your captain. Second, fire James Cobb, your drugged-out captain."

19. nunc *tempo: allegro*

I fall forward, grabbing the throat halyard to check my fall to the deck. Two passengers do fall to their knees. The sound rings like a broken bell. I look at Joe. He is on the helm, standing stock still. Kieran runs forward. He's waving over his shoulder. "Head up, head up." I feel the schooner turn into the wind.

There's been a collision, and we've lost our way. Joe heads into the wind. Sails luff.

"Okay, people let's gather at the galley hatch. Each of you is to grab a life jacket." I open the lockers and hand them out. "No, put it on."

"What's going on?" passengers ask repeatedly, gathering around me. I rally them by my galley hatch.

"I'll be slightly rude now and apologize later. Please put your life jacket on now. And sit on the hatch. I don't know anything more than you." I do see David swinging down into the fo'c'sle.

"There is nothing to worry about." Well, there maybe something to worry about. But really, there isn't. "We are fine. I'll tell you when to panic. You are officially allowed to be anxious. I'll grant that. We are a long way from panicking. Sit tight."

With deliberate calm, I walk forward. Kieran is leaning over the port bow. He turns toward the helm. He whistles to Joe, making the *travelling* movement with his hands and fingers, each spinning in circles. I hear the diesel engines start.

"Mags, get the sails down." The imperative is stingingly clear. I turn toward the starboard bow. I drop one halyard after the other. I open the figure eights one after the other and drop the halyards, letting the head sails fall on their own.

"I need two of you. One, two." I point to two passengers. I drop the foresail's halyards to the deck. "We're going to lower this. Don't drop it, and don't let it run through your hands. You'll burn. Use the belaying pin as your break. I'll be on the throat. Don't drop the peak too much faster than I drop the throat, okay?"

I undo the peak halyard, the lighter of the two. I leave one figure eight in place. "Take this." I hand over the tail. I undo the throat halyard. "Ready?" I speak softly. I see them nod. "Go." Sails drop. We douse the foresail with skill and speed. I take the halyards and make quick eights on the belaying pin. "Main halyards . . . " I point to my little team.

Stuart is tapping on the hull with his knife while pointing off the port side.

I take my eyes from his to watch my group move. I take in the slack from the foresail sheet.

"Same process, okay?" I drop the peak halyard neatly to the deck. One of my team follows my lead by laying the coils of the throat halyard to the deck as well.

"Yes." They have one figure eight left.

"Remember, this is heavier than the foresail. Ready?"

"Yes."

"Go." We drop the main with some speed.

Stuart has binoculars to his eyes. He studies the water off the port side. I move toward the bowsprit. I need to finish bringing the headsails down. I grab three bungees from a deck box. These are nice, bright yellow ones. I gather headsails by the armload and just bungee them haphazardly together. My effort won't survive much of a blow, but the sails aren't likely to climb the rigging. They are not going to swirl and tangle sheets. I put my hand on Kieran's back when I come off the bowsprit.

"We've hit a container." I know him to mean the large modular shipping containers that are used on ships, trucks, and rail cars. "I think we're taking in water. I want you on the wheel and the radio. Send Joe forward. Have Stuart go to my cabin and issue radios. I need one. I'll meet you on channel eight. If someone is on it, jump to seventy-two. Okay?"

I walk back through the waist and the passengers. "Folks, it will be a little while before we have an update. Apparently, we hit a submerged shipping container — one of these huge metal containers that are forty feet long. They have the ability to float a foot or two below the water level. The captain is assessing the damage. We did hit with a bit of force. If you don't mind, hang tight here a little longer. Maybe in a few minutes, we can spread out and some can come to the quarter deck. For now, though, just hang tight."

I have a small, handheld marine radio in my hand. The schooner's radio is tuned to channel sixteen. I watch the ship's motion toss duffle bags and foul-weather gear out of the fo'c'sle hatch.

"Mags. One, steer to stay with container as best as you can. Two, prepare to make a securité call."

"Stay with container. Standby to make call to Coasties. Got it. I am going to send a passenger forward to help stack those bags neatly."

"Right. Out."

"Thomas." I pick a name from my memory of the manifest. In the short three hours since breakfast, I have few names firm in my mind. Rachel and Thomas are all I can remember of the nine people on deck in front of me. "Thomas, can you please step aft?" He comes at me with a gentle run. I shout, "Slow down!" my hand in the universal *slow-down* motion.

"Thomas, can you step forward? Help stack those bags neatly. Your objective is to put them in such a way that we have easy access to move fore and aft. And we need access to the lines. So put them against the bulwarks. Okay?"

He nods and starts walking forward. "Thomas? Thomas," I beckon him.

"There is a bit of a courtesy here. I'm not being mean. We're not in a rush. Things are fine. Just move deliberately. No running. When someone on the boat asks you do something, please acknowledge it verbally. It is even often appropriate to repeat your instructions. Okay?"

"Yes."

"Thanks."

"One more thing, this is still your vacation. You are allowed to have a little fun, even emergencies can be fun, right?"

"Yes, ma'am."

"Head forward, then." I haven't been called ma'am in over three years. "Rachel?" She is getting called because she is the other name that I know. "Rachel, can you come aft?" She stands.

She walks toward me, looking over the starboard side.

"Do you see it?"

"Yes I do. That's huge."

"About half our size and who knows how heavy. Listen, can you help me a bit back here? I need another pair of hands."

"Sure. I can help."

"Good. You did a nice job on the lines this morning."

"Thanks." She smiles with little lines around her eyes.

"There's a clipboard hanging at the bottom of the aft companionway. Can you scoot down and get that? Make sure the pen works too."

"Sure."

I make notes of our position, reading lat and long from the GPS. I start tracking the time. I build a small log of activity working, backwards to the impact. I note that gear from the fo'c'sle is being evacuated to the deck. My supposition is that the removal of the gear from the fo'c'sle indicates one of two situations: one, they are trying to find a hole, or two, they found a hole.

"Rachel, your next job is to keep an eye on that container. I need to keep it in sight. Okay?"

"Sure."

"So if we drift away from it, tell me. I'll kick us into gear. Right now I'm going to make a call to the Coast Guard. This is not a Mayday call. There are three levels of calls that vessels make when communicating problems. We are going to make a priority three type call. It will simply be to inform the US Coast Guard that a hazard exists. I just don't want you to be alarmed by the nature of the call."

"Bridge, Captain?" I use my handheld to call Kieran.

"Go."

"Wet or dry?"

"Damp?"

"'Kay. I'll call the Coasties."

"Good."

I put the handheld down and take the mic from the mounted radio. "Say-curitay, say-curitay, say-curitay. This is the schooner Black Swan . . . " I report the submerged container, our location, and fourteen souls.

"Black Swan, this is US Coast Guard, are you reporting damage? Over."

"Not now. Damage assessment underway with captain and first mate. We struck on our starboard bow. We are steel hulled schooner with several watertight compartments. I will update as needed."

"Sailing vessel Black Swan, US Coast Guard. Change and answer twenty-one alpha."

"Black Swan on two-one alpha."

"What do you estimate the direction and speed of the container's drift to be?"

"Stand by." I look toward Rachel, "Rachel?"

"Yes."

"How are we doing on the container?"

"It's there. I'm having trouble seeing it."

"Point and keep your finger firmly on it."

"Okay."

I engage the engine. I ease the throttle forward. I turn starboard, watching the container come alongside. We are separated by twenty yards and parallel now. I ghost along, then pull back to neutral. I wait. The ribbed container is clearer to me now. It appears brown below the water. I guess its original color to be red.

"Sailing vessel Black Swan, US Coast Guard on twenty-one alpha."

"Black Swan, go," I answer. I am thinking they don't know what the phrase "stand by" means. I envision blue uniformed Coasties in a dark dispatch room, crowded by computer consoles, radio consoles, and displays of coastlines. I have never seen one, but I have seen operations control centers. They can't be too different. There sits a young, enlisted guy with a bit of action. He probably doesn't have anything much to do.

"Black Swan, please report your location."

I read latitude and longitude to the third decimal from the GPS display. "US Coast Guard, Black Swan, our drift appears east at four knots."

"Black Swan, US Coast Guard, acknowledge container drift is at four knots at zero-niner-zero."

"Roger, US Coast Guard. Black Swan will be monitoring channel twenty-one alpha. Out." I offer a gentle "shut up." I hit the monitor sixteen button and the scan button.

"Helm?" I pick up the handheld.

I answer Kieran, "Helm, go."

"Wet."

"Right, wet."

"Head towards the barn. Go with Plan Wet for now, too."

"Plan Wet, aye."

I put the throttle forward, turning slowly to port. I point us toward home. "Rachel, can you round up the rest and bring them aft?"

"Okay."

They gather quietly around the wheel. "Folks, we're going to change our plans. First, I need to see in front of me. Please step around to both sides. Can you all hear me?" I continue without a reply. "We've hit a partially submerged container. These bastards can weigh as much as twenty to thirty tons. There is a small rupture forward in the starboard bow. We can't continue, so we are going back home. We will refund your money, and we can help you find fun stuff to do in the area. I am deeply sorry about this experience. We are all safe. There is a watertight compartment forward, and we have ample pumps. There is no more risk of sinking now than there was when we left the dock. That said, we are going to take a few precautions.

"It will be some hours before we get to the dock. The trip back will be slower than the trip out. For now, we'll run with the engines. Speed will increase the pressure on the area, and that would be bad.

"I'll ask you all to remain on deck. At some point, we can take off the life jackets. Not yet, not for a little while. Right now, I'd like you to organize in twos. You'll check in with Rachel, my new assistant, before you go below. Please pack your stuff and place it on the galley table for now. When you are back on deck, tell Rachel and she'll—"

"US Coast Guard to sailing vessel Black Swan on twenty-one alpha."

"Go for Black Swan on two-one alpha."

"Black Swan, US Coast Guard, please advise on damage assessment."

"US Coast Guard, please stand by."

"Black Swan, US Coast Guard, please report radio operator's name."

"US Coast Guard, Black Swan. My name is Margaret Noonan. I am the second mate of record for the schooner Black Swan. I am also a licensed master with a sailing endorsement. Please stand by for five minutes."

"Black Swan, US Coast Guard, standing by and monitoring channel twenty-one alpha."

Again addressing my passengers, I continue: "Okay, in twos. Go below, pack neatly, and put your kit on the table. Cabin one first."

When Rachel is done recording names, I say, "Note the time, eleven eighteen. Then, can you duck below and get my life jacket? It's in the locker, kitty corner from my bunk." My life jacket is designed for yacht racing. It fits well and provides great range of motion. I have a knife, a whistle, a strobe, and sundry gear all tethered to it.

I make a call to Kieran for details on the handheld radio. I secure myself to my life vest. With a forced smile, I pick up the microphone for the bigger radio.

"US Coast Guard, schooner Black Swan on two-one alpha with damage report, Break. US Coast Guard, Black Swan. We have struck a forty-by-eight-foot shipping container. The container was partially submerged when we struck her with our starboard bow. There is a three-sided dimple in the steel. The captain is reporting a minor hole of a few inches." He actually said it looked like the steel tore. "We are attempting to bung the hole. Break." I take a breath and think through my next statements. "The damaged area is within a forward watertight compartment. The captain reports that our pumps will be able to keep the vessel dry. We have several pumps on board, including auxiliary, portable pumps. We are returning to our home berth with the fourteen souls. All souls are wearing type one life jackets. There is no expectation for further problems. Over."

"Black Swan, US Coast Guard. You are reporting damage to your hull. You are taking on small amounts of water. And you do not require assistance, is that correct? Over."

"US Coast Guard, Black Swan. That is correct. We are not requiring assistance. We have the problem well in hand."

"Black Swan, US Coast Guard, please continue to monitor channel twenty-one alpha. US Coast Guard out."

Water pours out of the primary bilge pump. It streams out for a minute, then stops.

"Helm, Captain." Again, I pick up the portable radio.

"Go ahead, Mags."

"Hey Captain, when you can free someone, send him back. I should take ten minutes for Plan L."

"Right. Good." Plan L is something we've planned, prepared for, and never had to do.

Stuart starts his walk back. His shirt is soaked. His hair is soaked. "I'll bring up some coffee. You've got the helm. One-ninety-five."

"One-nine-five, aye."

"Rachel, can you join me?"

Together, we crawl down to the galley, down into my home. It is the same, warm, dry place it always is. Bags are piling on the table. Plan L is our plan for lifeboat evacuation. Each of the deployable lifeboats has kits within. But I have supplement kits in plastic tubs. They include food, water, a few useful tool-like knives, fishing gear, radios, batteries, lasers, and wool blankets. One is stowed in the forward bench of the galley table, the toughest seat to get to. I walk across the furniture and pull up the cushions and the plywood base. I pull out one, then two purple plastic tubs. These are like over-sized Tupperware, sealed with duct tape. On the tape, I have written *MN 15MAR04*. I pack them each year, never expecting to use them.

Rachel and I get them to the deck. I then pour coffee for Stuart.

I hand him his coffee. "Why don't you get the two Plan L boxes from the aft cabins and change clothes?"

"Sure."

"I've got the helm."

Without our new schooner, Raven, ready for sea, we'll have to shut operations down for a while, at least cancel the next trip. Hopefully, we can call people before they leave their homes. They'll be disappointed that they won't sail with us this year on Black Swan.

Raven will need the winter to complete her rigging and shake down cruises. Tad and I will need the winter to supplement our crew and train a larger staff. By spring, we'll have two matching black schooners sailing between Maine and Canada.

It was a simple question: *How do I ask you to stay?* Tad asked me to stay. I asked him to hire Kieran. Together we tacked, changing our course.

Real smugglers would have found a way to lasso that container and drag it to a shallow spot during high tide. Who knows what may be found in there? — thousands of expensive Nike shoes, a race car, thirteen-liter per gallon flush toilets, drugs.

Ah well, we're not really here to smuggle. Not anymore, that is.

I discovered early on that sailing with others is far more fun than sailing alone. I'll leave those long solos for the loners. Me, I prefer a boat that is rich with stories, characters, and song. I like a warm galley, good food, and interesting people.

I unabashedly trespassed on the good people who run legitimate operations on the coast of Maine. During my years, I have known some of these schooners, their owners, and crew. Although some may hint at a shady ancient past, these people run terrific schooners. The Black Swan and Raven are completely fictitious. The crew, as you met them, manifested only for this novel.

Windjamming on the coast of Maine is a beautiful adventure. Under gray weather, the food will be warm and rich. With a crisp breeze and a clear sky, sailing the waters of Penobscot Bay is an experience for a lifetime.

If you have any questions about this fleet and the adventures they offer, contact the Maine Windjamming Association or visit their website at ***www.sailmainecoast.com***. After a trip or two, you'll join the rest of the sailors who can't cleave fiction from fact.

For the younger sailors

I would like to encourage the readers of *The Black Swan* to support community sailing wherever the programs are found: The Milwaukee Community Sailing Center, The Katchemak Bay Wooden Boat Show, or the Community Boating Group on the Charles River in Boston. There are organizations throughout the US. These programs introduce kids to adventure and water with safety and guidance. There's a national guide on the US Sailing website.

There are several programs for training at sea on Tall Ships. The best known of these is The American Sail Training Association, ***www.tallships.sailtraining.org.***

About the Author

Christina Moore is a native of New England, a place she has called home yet been separated from most of her adult life. She first sailed as a child on New England waters and subsequently joined Community Boating, Inc. There, she learned to sail on small boats on the Charles River. In the decades that followed, Christina has sailed on schooners and tall ships at irregular intervals, working as a sailor or cook. During her ten years in Alaska, there was a short and horrible ninety-day stint on a vessel in the Gulf of Alaska and the North Pacific. That experience gave rise to the foundation of this book. Although the events of this novel bear little resemblance to that tour, her sense of isolation, misery, and illness resonate in *The Black Swan*.

Ashore, Christina works as a telecommunications engineer. Even in these positions, she seeks adventure and prefers offices with unusual views. The view from the office in the Midwest stretched over the yacht club where she raced several days a week. In Anchorage, she watched the sun swing around Sleeping Lady and Denali while she deployed systems for the health organizations in rural Alaska.

Christina has moved back to New England.

About the Illustrator

Laura Boles Faw was born and raised in Atlanta, Georgia. She received a degree in Art History from the University of the South in Sewanee, Tennessee. Laura has worked as an artist in a variety of media including painting, printmaking, and sculpture. In addition to her studio work, Laura has illustrated several books. She currently lives and works in San Francisco, California.

Credits

Editor	Kristy Lin Billun San Francisco
Illustrator	Laura Boles Faw San Francisco
Cover Art	Laura Boles Faw San Francisco
Sounding Board	Ann Little Newbury Anchorage & Woods Hole
Layout Editor	Susan Aiken Mcdonald Lincoln, MA

www.ingramcontent.com/pod-product-compliance
Lightning Source LLC
LaVergne TN
LVHW091053080826
845145LV00002B/732

* 9 7 8 0 9 7 9 1 5 6 2 0 5 *